URBAN WINGS
NO LIMITS ✈ JUST SKIES

```
I0525822
```

If you know someone who needs to read this book, share it forward. And if you're holding it now, know this: you already have what it takes.

I'm on a mission to inspire 500,000 young minds to step into STEM and soar into the industries of drones, aviation, aerospace, and urban mobility."

You're next. Let's fly.

No Limits, Just Skies!
#UrbanWingsCrew

PUBLISHED BY

DMJ MEDIA GROUP, LLC
Indianapolis, Indiana

What people are saying about
Urban Wings: No Limits, Just Skies

"I love reading stories about dreamers who lift each other up, just like the characters in this book. Their determination to chase their goals despite adversity, with the guidance of a men- tor, really resonated with me. It reminded me of how my friends, and I pushed each other to reach new heights with our drones."

– Josh Ward, Certified Drone Pilot

***

"I remember being a little girl in Haiti, watching airplanes high in the sky and dreaming of flying. This book took me back to those dreams and is a wonderful read for young people who dare to dream of taking flight. It's a reminder that with dedication, anything is possible."

-Krista Saint Dic, Commercial Airline Pilot

***

The platonic chemistry created at the beginning of the story between Freddie, Genesis, and Miah exemplifies the duality of friendships and dreams. Their eagerness and yet realistic fear towards making their dreams reality, lifts off the pages and into the reader's consciousness. It makes one think; what are your true limitations?

The reality is, dreams do take resources. The authors explores and develops themes of real-life struggles that plague under-resourced populations. Things like money, drugs, and generational cycles.

Flying drones allows Freddie, Genesis, and Miah to escape the fear of the future. The author describes it as a "slice of peace"

This story is about becoming. It is about overcoming real life hindrances of environmental stressors and restrictions. The characters, themselves, learn to "fly."

-Christini Green

Urban Wings: No Limits, Just Skies

*Can Freddie, Miah, and Genesis overcome obstacles, chase their
aviation dreams, and prove that determination can soar beyond doubt?*

I want to express my deepest gratitude to the incredible remote and commercial pilots, flight attendants, dispatchers, crew schedulers, and aviation maintenance professionals who continue to inspire the next generation to explore careers in aviation.

Your willingness to share your personal journeys shines a light on the vast opportunities across the many pathways in aviation and serves as a powerful reminder of the extraordinary individuals at the heart of the industry who generously give their time to mentor youth.

It has been a true privilege to hear your stories and witness your passion and dedication in action. Your words to youth and their families have more impact than you may ever realize.

Thank you for being a beacon of inspiration and hope for so many.

Special thanks to Beth Warren aka Beth by Design, the brilliant book cover designer whose typography brought the title to life. Your eye for detail and creativity helped capture the spirit of this story in just a glance.

-DMJ

DMJ Media Group, LLC
Indianapolis, Indiana

Dayna Offutt Digital Designs
Indianapolis, Indiana

Library of Congress Registration Number: TXu2-453-426
Copyright © 2024 Darrell Earnest Morton, Jr.

Story by: Darrell E. Morton, Jr.
Front & Back Cover by: Roshanay@illustrationhiv
Edited by: Erin Naylor & Dayna Offutt

Rights and Permissions: Darrell
Ernest Morton, Jr.
Email: darrellmortonjr@gmail.com ISBN:

978-0-9858687-3-4

Dedication

To my cousin, Marvin Barlow, an Air Force veteran, a man of brilliance, resilience, and unwavering dedication. Your intellect inspired, your talents amazed, and your determination set a standard for excellence. You served with honor, walked through life with quiet strength, and left behind a legacy of faith, service, and purpose. Though you have departed this world, the imprint of your wisdom, kindness, and sacrifice will forever remain in the lives you touched.

-DMJ

CONTENTS

1

THE DREAM

The rooftop was their spot, no question. High up, above the grind, the noise, the streets that didn't love nobody. Up here, it was just the three of them: Freddie, Miah, and Genesis, and the sky stretched out big and wide like it was waiting for them. Freddie stood on the edge, the toes of his new J's hangin' off the ledge like he was daring gravity to come at him.

"Man, y'all ain't even gon' be able to see me up there," Freddie said, arms spread wide like wings. "I'mma be up so high, you gon' need a telescope just to spot me."

"Boy, please." Miah leaned back on the busted AC unit, arms crossed like she owned the place. "You ain't even passed math yet, talkin' 'bout flyin' planes. By the time you take off, I'll be smokin' past you in my fighter jet. Real speed. Not that slow paper-airplane stuff."

Freddie cut his eyes at her, smirking. "Keep talkin', Miah. I'll see you in my rearview."

"Ain't no rearview in a jet, dummy," Miah shot back, grinning.

They went back and forth like that all the time, throwing shade and big talk, but it was all love. Up here, they could say the wildest things, dream the biggest dreams, and nobody could tell them any different. Freddie looked over at Genesis, lying flat on the rooftop like she was staring into outer space.

"What about you, G? What's next for you?"

Genesis didn't answer right away. She stayed quiet, the kind of quiet that made you lean in just to catch what she might say. Finally, she sat up, her arms wrapped around her knees. "Tuskegee," she said, her voice soft but solid. "My grandpa used to tell me about it, about the airmen, how they broke barriers. Now they got a aviation program. I'm gon' be part of that. Carry the legacy. For him. For us."

Freddie nodded his head. "You already got it all mapped out, huh?"

Miah nodded, her usual tough-girl smirk swapped out for something real. "That's dope, Gen. For real. I can see you doin' that."

They both admired Genesis' clarity. She had a specific goal, a legacy to live up to. The moment hung between them, charged with hope. But down on the streets below, it wasn't so simple. Bills piled up at home, classes weren't getting easier, and expectations seemed to grow heavier by the day. Up here, though, those worries faded.

"You ever think 'bout it?" Freddie asked, his voice lower now. "Like, what it's really gon' feel like? Bein' up there for real? Lookin' down on all this?" He waved a hand over the city below. "Like, all this don't even matter no more."

Genesis tilted her head, her face serious. "Yeah, I think about it. But sometimes... sometimes I wonder what happens if it don't work out. What if life just..." She stopped, her voice catching. "What if it keeps throwin' stuff at us? What if we can't make it?"

Miah leaned over, elbowing her like she was tryin' to knock the doubt right out of her. "Nah, don't think like that, Gen. We got this. We gotta get this. We already fightin' to be here. Ain't no turnin' back now."

Freddie didn't say much, just nodded like he was tryin' to convince himself too. That fear was real, though, the kind that crept in late at night when the world got too quiet. What if the dreams were too big? Too far? What if the weight of everything was too much to shake off?

But Genesis met his eyes, steady and strong. "We gon' figure it out," she said. "We have to."

The three of them sat there in the stillness, the city hummin' below, the sky stretching on above. Up here, their dreams felt like they were right there, just close enough to grab. But they knew the climb to get there wasn't gonna be easy.

2

LIFE ON THE GROUND

Next morning, Freddie stood at the bottom of his building, looking up at that rooftop where he, Miah, and Genesis had been dreaming just hours before. The early sun spilled gold over the skyline, making the city almost look peaceful for once. For a second, he could almost feel it again, the breeze, the calm, like the world is not so heavy when you're up high.

He closed his eyes, letting that feeling wash over him. Up there, man, it was like the sky didn't have any limits. Their problems? They were specks of dust compared to that wide-open horizon. It was weightless, like for once, they could breathe.

But real life didn't wait. Freddie took a deep breath, pushed the thoughts aside, and began the long, familiar walk to U-Street High. As he got closer, the sounds of the school day crept in, muffled at first, then louder with every step. The moment he swung open the main entrance door, the noise hit him full force: lockers slamming, voices overlapping, the chaotic rhythm of students moving, talking, hustling. The rooftop's quiet felt like a distant world, one he had already left behind.

Stepping through the doors, the buzzing fluorescent lights smacked him right in the face. They couldn't hold a candle to the sunrise he'd just left behind. The smell of burnt toast from the cafeteria mixed with that lemony cleaning stuff that the janitors used. Routine. Stale. Same ol', same ol'.

Freddie slid through the crowded hallway, dodging elbows and side- eyes, his mind still stuck on the rooftop.

"Yo, Freddie!"

Big Rodney's voice boomed through the chaos, loud and clownin' like always. They had been tight for years, longtime teammates on the baseball team through elementary and middle school. But things started shifting once they hit high school. Freddie focused on aviation dreams, while Rodney got caught up in a different crowd.

"What's good?" Rodney called out, a slick grin on his face. "I got that ooowee lined up this weekend, what you tryna do?"

Freddie didn't even break stride. "Man, you know I ain't on that."

Rodney smirked, shaking his head. "Still got yo head in the clouds wit' them planes, huh? Keep dreamin', lil' bro. Bet you end up teachin' just like your ol' man. He didn't make it as a pilot, and you probably won't either."

Freddie rolled his eyes and kept walking, letting Rodney's words bounce off him. He wasn't about to let someone who had already given up on their own future talk him out of his.

By the time he slipped into science class, Mr. Barlow was already going in about the four forces of flight, Bernoulli's Principle, and something else Freddie couldn't catch. The rumor was Mr. Barlow used to be an Air Force pilot back in the day but due to a medical condition he had to stop flying and he left the military.

Freddie slouched in the back, trying to focus, but his eyes kept drifting to the flight charts hanging on the wall. Planes and numbers, arrows showing how air moved. His brain wasn't following, but his heart was already in the cockpit.

"Freddie!" Mr. Barlow's voice snapped him out of his trance. "You with us, or you up there flyin' already?"

Freddie sat up straight, playing it off with a grin. "Nah, I'm here. My bad, Mr. B."

Mr. Barlow raised an eyebrow but didn't push. Instead, his tone softened. "Dreamin' again?"

Freddie chuckled under his breath. "Ok, maybe."

The bell rang, signaling the end of class. Students hurriedly grabbed their books and backpacks, eager to move on to their next class. As they funneled toward the door, Mr. Barlow motioned for Freddie to stay back.

"Dreaming is good," he said, meeting Freddie's eyes. "But don't forget, it's the work that gets you there."

Freddie nodded slowly, taking that in. He wanted to brush it off, but the truth hit deep. Dreaming was the easy part. The grind, though? That's where the real fight was at.

3

BARRIERS

The weeks blurred into a haze of schoolwork and late-night rooftop talks, but the weight of their dreams pressed harder with each passing day. Freddie sat slouched against the rooftop wall, his open calculus book sprawled on the ground beside him. The bright red 'D' scrawled on his test paper glared at him like a taunt. He exhaled sharply, running a hand over his face.

"Man," he muttered to himself, "these numbers ain't nothin' but a setup to make me look stupid."

Miah leaned on the ledge, arms crossed, her vibe as sharp as her wit. "Nah, Freddie," she said with a smirk, "it's that 'D' on your test that's doin' that."

Freddie shot her a glare, half annoyed, half amused. "Oh, so that's what we doin' now? Cool. Ok."

Miah chuckled, her teasing tone softening. "C'mon, you know it's all love." She tilted her head toward the book. "But seriously, why you stressin' over math like this?"

"It's calculus," said Freddie as he rubbed the back of his neck, his voice tinged with frustration. "My dad's the one stressin' it. He's convinced I need it for pilot exams or some nonsense."

Miah rolled her eyes, sliding down to sit beside him. "Freddie, the math for those pilot exams is like basic stuff, geometry and a little trig maybe. You out here losin' sleep for no reason."

Freddie groaned, letting his head fall back against the wall. "Try tellin' my dad that. He's got this whole 'you gotta be prepared for anything' lecture on repeat. I'm drownin', Miah."

Across the rooftop, Genesis sat curled up, her arms wrapped around her knees. She wasn't laughing. She stared out at the distant city skyline, her silence heavy. "It's not just school for me, Freddie," she said softly, her voice carrying a weight that made both Freddie and Miah turn to her. "It's everything."

Freddie straightened, his frustration momentarily forgotten. "What's goin' on, G?"

She hesitated, chewing her bottom lip, before finally speaking. "My mom's got laid off from work. Bills are pilin' up, and... I don't know how I'm supposed to leave for Tuskegee. That's if I even get accepted, when everything here is fallin' apart. Feels real selfish even thinkin' about it."

The words hung in the air, heavier than the late fall breeze. Miah slid closer, her usually cool demeanor softening. "Genesis, it's not selfish to have dreams. You're allowed to want this for yourself."

Genesis shook her head, her jaw tightening as her voice cracked. "Dreams don't pay the light bill, Miah. What if I go and stuff gets worse? What if they need me here and I'm off chasin' somethin' that... that might not even work out anyway?"

Miah didn't respond right away. She stared at the skyline like it might hold the answers, her voice quieter when she finally spoke. "I get it. My dad thinks flyin' jets is reckless. Says it's too risky, too dangerous, especially for me."

Freddie frowned, confusion crossing his face. "Especially for you? What's that mean?"

Miah shrugged, her nonchalance betrayed by the crack in her voice. "'Cause I'm a girl. Says I should stick to somethin' safe, predictable. Somethin' that won't keep him up at night."

Freddie's frustration flared, his voice rising. "Man, that's trash. Your dad don't get it. He don't see what we see when we look up there."

Miah's smirk returned, but it was tinged with something deeper. "Yeah, well, he's not completely wrong. It is a risk. But every dream's a risk, right?"

Genesis looked down, her fingers fidgeting with one of her long braids. "What if we don't make it?" she whispered, the question hanging in the still night air.

The rooftop fell into silence, the weight of her words settling over them like a blanket. For a moment, even the city seemed to pause, the distant hum of traffic fading into the background.

Then Freddie laughed, loud and defiant, breaking the tension like shattering glass. "Man, forget all that," he said, his grin wide and contagious. "We'll figure it out. The math, the money, the doubts, all of it. We got to."

Genesis glanced at him, a small smile tugging at her lips. Miah nudged Freddie with her elbow, her smirk returning full force. "You talkin' real big for someone barely survivin' calculus."

Freddie grinned back, the tension finally breaking. "Hey, didn't say I'd figure it out alone. That's what y'all are here for."

Their laughter echoed across the rooftop, filling the air with something lighter than the heaviness they carried. For a brief moment, the city below felt less overwhelming, the stars above a little closer. Up here, it was easy to believe that their struggles didn't define them, that maybe, just maybe, they'd find a way to fly after all.

4

THE DRONE ZONE

After school let out, Freddie, Miah, and Genesis headed straight to their other spot, Mr. Barlow's so-called *"Drone Zone."* It wasn't much, just a chunk of the school parking lot roped off with some beat-up traffic cones, but to them, it was a training ground. The cracked asphalt made every landing an adventure, but Mr. Barlow said that just added "real-world conditions." They all knew it was code for "This is all the school budget could afford."

Miah grabbed one of the scuffed-up drones like it was her lifeline, her eyes lighting up with that laser focus she always had when she was in the zone.

"All right let's see what these busted-up joints can do," she said, powering one up and pulling the goggles down over her eyes.

For her, every lift-off was like getting closer to her dream of flying fighter jets. She let out a deep breath, eyes locked on the makeshift course ahead.

Freddie, though, held his controller tighter than usual, his frustration buzzing just under the surface. He watched Miah guide her drone through the cones, smooth as butter, while his felt like dead weight in his hands.

"I don't see how this old junk is supposed to teach us anything about flyin', and these goggles are trash," he grumbled, his voice cutting through the group with a sharp edge. It was the kind of tone that surfaced when the weight of the world felt just a little too heavy to bear. "Feels like everything I do lately just... ain't hittin' right."

Genesis paused, fiddling with her drone's settings. "What's up with you?" she asked, her tone half-concerned, half-annoyed. "You been trippin' all week."

Freddie sighed, his shoulders slumping under an invisible weight. "It's calculus," he admitted, the very word making him feel smaller. "I ain't gonna lie, I just can't keep up. The harder I study, the worse it gets. How am I supposed to pass this class, let alone learn how to really fly this thing?"

Mr. Barlow, who had been watching from the side, strolled over like he'd heard enough.

"Freddie," he said, leaning on the rickety table that held their gear, "you know what flying drones and calculus have in common?"

Freddie frowned. "That they both suck?"

Miah cracked up, but Mr. Barlow just shook his head with a grin. "Nah, man. They both take practice. Nobody's born knowing how to calculate the path of an aircraft or navigate a drone through high winds. You gotta mess up, figure it out, and keep goin'. That's the secret."

Freddie let out a weak laugh, but the frustration was still written all over his face.

"Great. Maybe I can put 'practiced really hard' on my transcript."

Miah cut in, her drone hovering in place like it was waiting for her cue.

"Trust me, I get it. You're fightin' calculus, I'm still fightin' my dad. Dude's convinced I'm gonna wake up one day and decide I don't wanna fly anymore. I am so tired of hearin', 'It's a reckless dream.'" She rolled her eyes. "Like, what does that even mean?"

Freddie smirked. "Your dad and Big Rodney should hang out. They'd have a lot to say about flyin'."

Miah laughed. "Facts. But here's the thing: they can doubt us all they want. We're still gonna prove 'em wrong."

Mr. Barlow nodded, his expression thoughtful. "Funny thing about dreams, sometimes people can't see your vision because they don't have one of their own. But that doesn't make yours any less real or worth chasing. Their doubts belong to them, not you."

Genesis stayed quiet, her hands steady on her controller. Finally, she said, "My mom still ain't got no job, and here I am, thinkin' about college tuition like it's no big deal. It's messin' me up."

Mr. Barlow put a hand on her shoulder, his voice softer now.

"Genesis, there's nothin' wrong with wantin' better for yourself. That guilt? That's proof you care. But you can't let it stop you. You're building the kind of grit and resilience that's gonna take you far. In fact, all of you are."

The three of them exchanged looks. It wasn't like their problems were gone, but somehow, they felt a little less heavy. Mr. Barlow had a way of making their struggles feel like part of the process instead of a roadblock.

Miah nudged Freddie with her elbow.

"Come on, bro. If we can keep these old drones from crashin', you can handle calculus. We got you."

Freddie leaned back with a smirk, eyeing Genesis. "You doin' my homework or what G?"

Genesis didn't even look up. "You tweakin', bro."

Miah grinned. "Patience, Freddie. Remember, have it, or become one." Freddie blinked. "What does that even mean?"

Miah chuckled. "I don't know. My dad says that to me all the time."

Freddie exhaled sharply, flicking the sticks on his controller. "Dead batteries," he muttered, frustration creeping into his voice. "This drone stuff is really startin' to get me twisted."

He yanked off the back of the controller and ripped out the drained batteries with a sharp tug, tossing them onto the table.

Nearby, Miah tightened her flight path, shutting out her dad's disapproval. Genesis steadied her drone, pouring all her worries about her mom into each precise movement, her focus unwavering.

Just as Freddie dug through his bag for replacements, Mr. Barlow's whistle cut through the air, snapping them all back to reality. Practice was over.

As they packed up, Mr. Barlow pulled them in close, his voice steady and sure.

"What y'all are doing here, it's bigger than drones. You're learning how to handle life. How to bounce back, how to trust yourselves, how to keep climbing no matter how rough the winds get. Hard times will come, and frustration will hit, but you have to remember, always be there for each other. No matter what."

He let his words settle, his gaze moving between them, making sure they truly heard him. Then, with a small smile, he tapped his phone.

"I capture every practice and every competition on video. Not just for technique, but so one day, when y'all look back, you can see just how much you've grown. Every stumble, every breakthrough, every moment that made you stronger."

He nodded, pride shining in his eyes.

"You're my urban wings, and you have no limits, just skies. And I'm here to make sure you never forget that."

Freddie let the words sink in as he zipped his backpack. The weight of the day still pressed on him, but something about Mr. Barlow's words loosened its grip.

As they stepped out of practice, their hearts felt as heavy as the gear slung over their shoulders. Their minds wiggled with dreams, some barely staying afloat.

But Freddie, Miah, and Genesis held onto that spark, the one thing that kept hope alive and pushed them forward.

The road ahead was long, uncertain, but with each other and their makeshift drone zone, they knew they could handle it.

5

CHALLENGES AT HOME

As the days rolled by, drone practice became the trio's little slice of peace. In those moments, it felt like the weight of the world slipped off their backs. But once practice ended and the real world crept back in, the struggles Freddie, Miah, and Genesis carried with them became harder to ignore.

Genesis felt it the most.

Every day, she watched her mom grind on the phone, chasing leads, trying to lock down a job. Every "no" on the other end of the line hit Genesis like a gut punch. It wasn't just her mom struggling, it was their whole household. And there was only so much Genesis could do. That frustration stayed locked up inside her, boiling just under the surface. What was a high school kid supposed to do against a stack of unpaid bills?

Late one night, Genesis sat alone at the kitchen table, the glow of her laptop screen casting shifting shadows across her face. A mountain of scholarship applications lay in front of her, but exhaustion blurred the words before she could process them.

The hum of the fridge was the only sound, until something else cut through the silence.

A soft, broken noise.

Muffled sobs.

Her chest tightened. The sound was coming from her mother's room.

Genesis' stomach twisted, her fingers tightening around the edge of the table. Had she been so caught up in deadlines and essays that she hadn't noticed how hard this was for her mom? Had she ever stopped to ask?

She blinked hard, forcing down the sting behind her eyes. For the first time, she realized college wasn't just changing her life. It was changing theirs. The late-night job searches, the bills piling up, the weight of trying to hold everything together.

And now, Genesis was about to add to that burden by chasing a dream they couldn't afford.

She wiped at her eyes, staring at the Tuskegee application on her screen. She thought, "Maybe I'm asking for too much. Maybe it's selfish to still want this."

A few minutes later, the soft shuffle of slippers broke the silence.

Genesis quickly straightened up as her mom entered the kitchen, her eyes tired but warm as she took in the cluttered table.

"You're up late again," her mom murmured, glancing at the stack of papers. "Still thinking about school?"

Genesis nodded, her fingers and palms sweaty.

"Yeah," she muttered, her voice barely above a whisper. "I just don't know how I'm gonna make this work."

She hesitated, then let the words spill out.

"I really wanna go to Tuskegee so bad, but... maybe it's too much to ask."

Her mom sighed and pulled out a chair beside her, placing a gentle hand on her shoulder.

"Genesis, listen to me," she said, her voice steady despite the weariness in her eyes. "We've always been a family that finds a way, no matter what. Losing my job doesn't change that, it just means we've got to lean into our strength even more.

"You're going to college! That's not a burden, baby, it's the dream we've been chasing together. You've got that fire in you, and I won't let you dim it.

"We'll figure this out. Together."

Again, Genesis nodded slowly, her throat tight as her mom's words sank in. She wanted to believe them. She needed to believe them. But as her mom stood and headed
back to bed, that whisper of doubt still lingered. Could she really pull this off? Was she enough?

The dim kitchen light flickered faintly, casting long shadows over the Tuskegee application on her screen. Genesis traced the edges with her finger; her gaze went to a notepad listing backup schools she'd been forced to consider.

Her heart felt heavy with the weight of it all. Tuskegee wasn't just her dream, it was a dream her mom and her siblings deserved to see come true. But the road there? It felt endless.

In the stillness of the kitchen, Genesis made herself a promise. No matter the setbacks, she wouldn't give up. She'd keep pushing, keep dreaming, keep working. This dream wasn't just hers, it was all of theirs.

6

MIAH'S MISERY

Miah could feel the fight brewing before her father even opened his mouth. The tension sat heavy in the air, thick and suffocating, as he leaned against the kitchen doorframe, arms crossed like he was preparing for battle. His voice was low, but the sharpness of his words cut through the quiet of the room.

"Miah, you've got a good head on your shoulders," he started, each word weighed down with judgment. "But you're wastin' it on this nonsense. Fighter jets? That's a man's job. Girls don't belong in the sky, riskin' their lives when they've got real responsibilities down here."

Miah's hands trembled as she pressed them to the top of her head, trying to hold herself together.

"Real responsibilities?" she shot back, her voice tinged with sarcasm but laced with hurt. "You mean, like setting the table and learning how to sew?" The words burned on her tongue. "Flyin' isn't reckless, Dad. It's my dream, and I'm gonna make it happen."

Her father shook his head, his frustration spilling over.

"A dream? That's all it is, a little girl's fantasy. Why can't you focus on somethin' practical, somethin' that makes sense? You should be thinkin' about nursing school or maybe being a teacher. That's what girls do, Miah."

They take care of people. They don't go chasin' after dangerous ideas that'll get 'em killed."

The words hit Miah like a slap, and her chest tightened.

"Why does it matter that I'm a girl?" she asked, her voice cracking under the weight of her frustration. "Why can't I want more? You think the only thing I'm good for is takin' care of other people?"

Her father sighed heavily, rubbing his temples like he was tired of even having the conversation.

"This ain't about what you're good for. It's about what's right. Flyin' jets? That's not right for a girl. You'll embarrass yourself, and us, tryin' to play in a man's world."

Miah's pulse raced, her anger bubbling over.

"You don't get it, Dad! I'm not tryin' to play at anything, I'm serious about this. Just because you don't believe in me doesn't mean I'm gonna stop."

"Serious?" His voice rose, sharp and biting. "What's serious is the danger, the risks, the failure waiting for you when you realize this ain't gonna work. You wanna end up like those fools on the news, crashing into the ocean? You think you're better than them?"

She stared at him, her jaw clenched and her fists tight.

"You'll see," she said quietly, her voice thick with venom. "One day, you'll see."

But he was already walking away, waving her off like she wasn't worth the energy.

"Yeah, well, don't come cryin' to me when you fall flat on your face."

Miah couldn't take it anymore. Grabbing her backpack, she stormed into her bedroom, slamming the door behind her. Her pulse pounded in her ears as she paced the small space, her breath quick and shallow.

This room was the only place where she could let the weight of her father's words fall away, where she could be alone with her dreams, even if no one else believed in them. She threw herself onto the bed, staring up at the ceiling, her eyes locking onto the posters of her heroes, Madeline Swegle, Shawn Kimbrell, and Theresa Claiborne. Women who had defied the odds and soared as military pilots.

Today, those faces seemed just a little farther away, their accomplishments feeling almost out of reach. The air in the room felt thick, offering none of the usual comfort it once had. Her father's voice echoed in her mind, refusing to be silenced.

A girl. That's all he sees me as. Just a girl.

Doubt crept in, the same way it always did, whispering that maybe he was right, that maybe she was reaching too far. She clenched her fists, gripping the blanket beneath her as she fought against his words. Then she thought of Freddie and Genesis, their laughter, their shared ambitions and a flicker of defiance sparked inside her.

No, this isn't just a dream. It's my future. And I'm gonna get there. She sat up, staring at the posters again, determination settling in her chest. She didn't know how she'd prove him wrong, but she swore to herself that she would.

One day, she'd rise above his doubts, above every cruel word, and make him eat them. For now, the posters were enough, a reminder of the skies that would one day be hers.

7

COMPETITION DAY

The day of the first drone competition had finally arrived, and the energy in the gymnasium was electric. Freddie, Miah, and Genesis stood just inside the entrance, their eyes scanning the chaotic scene. Teams bustled at their stations, last-minute adjustments buzzing like a hive of activity. The air was thick with the hum of drones, the squeak of sneakers on polished wood, and the chatter of spectators. Bright overhead lights cast sharp shadows, making the competition area feel larger and far more intimidating.

Across the room, Riverside Academy's team was setting up. Their sleek, state-of-the-art drones gleamed under the lights, while their matching uniforms made them look like a professional crew. In stark contrast, U-Street's team huddled around their patched-together drones, wearing plain, mismatched school-logo clothes that spoke of their outsider status. Miah's eyes lingered on Riverside's setup, her stomach twisting. "Wow," she spoke softly under her breath. "They're the best team in the city. We are so out of our league."

Freddie forced a smile, though his own nerves were twisting like knots in his gut.

"We practiced hard. We can do this, yo." Genesis adjusted her goggles and nodded firmly. "It ain't about how we look. It's about how we fly."

The rounds began, and the competition was fierce. Riverside breezed through the course with effortless precision, their drones slicing through the air like arrows. In contrast, U-Street's drones wobbled on their first flights, their patched-up propellers struggling to maintain balance under the bright lights.

Each successful turn brought a collective sigh of relief, and each near-miss sent their hearts racing. As the semi-final round approached, the tension was palpable. Freddie wiped his sweaty palms on his jeans, his jaw tight with concentration. Miah's hands trembled as she adjusted the drone's controls, the weight of her team's hopes pressing down on her. Genesis stood nearby, quietly muttering calculations under her breath.

Then disaster struck.

Miah's drone sputtered mid-air, veering sharply off course. She barely had time to react before a loud crack echoed through the gym. The drone slammed into a barrier, the plastic frame snapping under the strain of the high-speed turn. Gasps rippled through the spectators as the broken pieces clattered to the floor.

Flying too fast had put too much stress on the frame, causing it to snap apart. Miah's shoulders slumped, her hands falling to her sides. She stared at the wreckage, her chest tightening. Her voice came out as a whisper, barely audible over the commotion.

"That's it. We're done."

Freddie crouched beside the broken drone without hesitation, his face set with determination.

"We're fixin' it," he said firmly, looking to Genesis for reassurance. "We ain't done yet."

Genesis dropped to her knees, gathering scattered pieces with careful hands.

"Come on, let's go, let's go," she said, her voice steady despite the doubt gnawing at her edges. "We're a team, and teams don't give up."

Miah pushed the goggles up onto her head and froze, her gaze fixed on the broken drone. Her vision blurred with tears of frustration, but she quickly blinked them away. Taking a deep breath, she crouched down beside her teammates, determination replacing doubt.

"Alright," she said firmly. "Let's do this."

The three worked quickly, their hands moving with urgency and precision. The patched-up drone looked rough, its cracks hastily sealed with tape, its propellers slightly bent but it was theirs, and it was ready to fly again.

The final round loomed, the course stretching out before them like a gauntlet of impossibility. It was the toughest challenge they had faced yet: tight turns, steep climbs, and narrow gates that demanded both precision and speed.

Freddie's grip tightened on the controls, his gaze locked on the course through his goggles. As the countdown ended, he guided the drone into the first sharp bend. The propellers hummed perilously close to the barrier, but with a quick adjustment and steady nerves, he pulled it through just in time.

Miah followed, her movements cautious but steady. She held her breath with each turn, her patched-up drone wobbling slightly but holding its course.

Genesis brought up the rear, her drone gliding smoothly, her calculated adjustments keeping their pace consistent. They weren't perfect, but they pressed forward, determined to finish strong. When they finally crossed the finish line, the three of them let out a collective sigh of relief. The gym erupted in applause for the top teams, but U-Street wasn't among them. They huddled together, glancing at the scoreboard as the final rankings appeared.

Fifth place.

Silence hung between them for a moment as they processed the result. It wasn't the victory they had dreamed of, but it wasn't a loss either. Freddie let out a deep breath, a grin forming across his face.

"Fifth place out of thirty teams, I'll take it," he said, nudging Miah. "Not bad for a bunch of outsiders."

Miah laughed, the tension in her shoulders easing. "Yeah, it's cool, but next time we takin' first."

Genesis smiled softly, her gaze lingering on the scoreboard.

"We showed them all that we belong here," she said, her voice steady with resolve. "Yeah, next time we walkin' out with that first-place hardware."

As they stepped out of the gym, the weight of the day began to fade, replaced by something stronger, hope. Fifth place wasn't the end; it was a beginning, a foundation to build on. They weren't just competitors, they were outsiders, which meant they had to think differently, push harder, and outwork everyone else.

8

THE STRUGGLE IS REAL

After the high of the drone competition, life returned to its usual rhythm. For Freddie, Miah, and Genesis, "normal" didn't feel so normal anymore.

They'd tasted progress, felt the spark of potential, but their personal struggles were still there, waiting to trip them up at every turn. For Freddie, calculus remained his biggest roadblock.

Every failed quiz hit like a gut punch, stacking into a wall between him and his dream of becoming a pilot. It wasn't just about numbers on a page. This felt personal. Like the universe was testing him, asking if he was really good enough.

Night after night, he sat at his desk, staring at equations that twisted and turned, mocking him with their complexity. One night, after what felt like the hundredth attempt to solve the same problem, Freddie snapped. He grabbed his notebook and flung it across the room. It hit the wall with a dull thud, pages scattering like autumn leaves in the wind.

"Man, I can't do this," he muttered, his voice quivering with frustration. He pressed his hands against his face, fingers covering his eyes. The knot in his chest tightened, pulling him under.

His mom appeared in the doorway, leaning against the frame with her arms crossed. Concern softened her expression.

"Freddie, what's goin' on?" she asked, her voice calm but firm. Freddie slumped in his chair, shaking his head. "I'm just not cut out for this, Mom," he said, the words spilling out before he could stop them. "How am I supposed to fly a plane if I can't even pass a stupid quiz?"

His mom stepped inside, pulling up a chair next to him. She placed a gentle hand on his shoulder. "Baby, you're pushin' yourself too hard. You've got this, you just need to take it one step at a time."

Freddie hesitated before asking, "Mom, can I ask you somethin'? Of course, baby. What's on your mind?"

He glanced down, rubbing his hands together. "If you and Dad knew I wanted to be a pilot, why'd he make me take calculus? I don't even need it."

His mom chuckled, shaking her head. "That's somethin' you'll have to ask your dad when he gets home from work."

Freddie raised an eyebrow. "You tryna get me killed, Mom? Ain't no way I'm askin' your husband that, you *know* how he is."

She burst out laughing, the sound filling the room. "Your Dad just wanted you to have options, Freddie. He's always thinkin' about a backup plan, in case flyin' doesn't work out."

Freddie frowned. "Why do parents always doubt their kids?"

His mom's expression softened. "It's not doubt, baby. It's called life experience," she said gently. "We just want the best for you. And right now? That means stickin' with calculus."

Freddie let out a heavy sigh. "But what if I can't? What if I'm just not smart enough?"

His mom scooted closer, her tone turning serious. "Let me tell you something," she said. "When I was your age, chemistry had me feelin' the same way. I thought I'd never get it. But then I got a tutor, someone who showed me how to look at it differently. Once I stopped trying to force it, the pieces started to fit."

Freddie stared at the mess of papers on his desk. "What if a tutor doesn't work for me?" he asked, his voice barely above a whisper.

His mom tilted his chin up, her gaze locking with his. "Struggles don't mean you're not built for something. They mean you're still building," she said. "Ain't no shame in needin' help; what matters is you don't quit."

Freddie chewed on her words, feeling a flicker of hope in the midst of his doubt. "You think a tutor can really help me see it differently?" he asked hesitantly.

His mom nodded. "I know it," she said. "But you gotta give yourself a chance. Don't let this struggle make you forget how far you've already come."

Freddie leaned back in his chair, staring at the papers on his desk. "Alright," he said, "I'll try a tutor but whoever it is, they better be a miracle worker."

His mom smiled, giving his shoulder a squeeze. "That's my boy. We'll figure this out together."

The doubts didn't vanish that night. They still lingered, whispering in the back of Freddie's mind. But for the first time in weeks, he felt like maybe, just maybe, he wasn't fighting this battle alone. And that small spark of determination? It was enough to keep him going.

9

GENESIS' TURNING POINT

Genesis had been burning the midnight oil for weeks. Her laptop glowed in the dimly lit room, casting long shadows over stacks of papers, half-filled notebooks, and scholarship applications sprawled across the table. The bags under her eyes told the story of sleepless nights and relentless hustle.

Every rejection email hit like a gut punch, but she refused to let them stop her. Tuskegee University wasn't just a school, it was her dream, her ticket to a future bigger than anything she had ever known. She wasn't about to give up. Not now, not ever.

Hunched over the table, head in her hands, she let out a deep sigh as her laptop pinged with yet another email. Before she could bring herself to open it, the soft shuffle of slippers against the floor signaled her mother's approach.

"Baby, you've been at this all night again?" Her mom's voice was gentle but heavy with concern.

Genesis rubbed her temples but didn't look up. "Feels like every time I get somewhere, another rejection comes through. I can't stop, though, Mom. I have to figure this out." Her mom stood over her, studying her in silence for a long moment, her face a mix of pride and worry. Then, she leaned in, placing a warm hand over Genesis'.

"Genny, let me tell you something about this family," she said, her voice steady. "We come from a long line of fighters, of dreamers who didn't stop when things got hard.

Your great-granddaddy came to this country with nothing but the clothes on his back and marched for his rights with nothing but his feet and his faith. And your uncle? He put himself through college working double shifts at the steel mill.

And you? You're out here making history in your own way. You're showing your little brother and sister what's possible. You're carving out a path they can follow."

Genesis swallowed hard, her mom's words pressing deep into her heart.

"Baby, I see how hard you're working, how much you want this," her mom continued. "You're proving that no matter where we come from, our dreams are worth fighting for.

And I know it gets tough, I know the rejections sting, but don't let them tell you what you can't do.

You are more than enough, Genesis. You always have been."

For the first time in days, Genesis felt some of the weight on her shoulders ease. Then, with a small smile, her mom reached into her robe pocket and pulled out an envelope.

"This came in the mail today. I didn't open it... figured I'd let you do the honors." Genesis froze, her eyes locking onto the envelope like it was a golden ticket.

The Tuskegee University logo stood out boldly, making her heart pound against her ribs. Hands trembling, she took the envelope from her mom and carefully tore it open. Her eyes darted over the letter, breath catching as the words leaped off the page.

"On behalf of Tuskegee University, we're thrilled to offer you a place in our aviation science program…" She read aloud, her voice shaking. Her head snapped up, eyes wide with disbelief.

"Mom… I got in. I really got in!"

Genesis leaped from her chair in excitement, nearly knocking it over as pure joy surged through her. Her mom's face lit up with a proud, knowing smile as she pulled Genesis into a tight hug.

"Of course, you did, baby girl! I knew you would."

Genesis clung to her mother, letting the relief and joy wash over her. Every late night, every moment of doubt, every rejection, it all faded into the background. But as the excitement settled, a new worry crept in. She pulled back, her expression shifting.

"But… how are we gonna pay for it?" she asked hesitantly. "This ain't cheap, and I don't want us drownin' in debt just because I got into my dream school."

Her mother squeezed her hands, her voice calm and unwavering. "We'll figure it out, Genny. We've faced harder things before, and we got through them. Don't let the 'how' stop you from celebrating the 'what.'

You worked for this, you earned it, and we're not lettin' money get in the way of what's meant for you."

Genesis bit her lip, her mind racing between practical fears and the letter in her hands, the proof of all she had overcome. Slowly, the doubt began to lift. She nodded, her voice soft but resolute. "You're right. I can't let this scare me. I'll keep pushin', keep applyin' for scholarships, keep workin'. I'm not givin' up, not on Tuskegee, and not on myself."

Her mom's smile widened, pride shining through tired eyes.

"That's my Genny. And remember, you're not alone in this. We'll tackle it together, one step at a time."

For the first time in weeks, Genesis let herself truly smile. A real one. Full and unforced. The path ahead was still uncertain, still full of challenges, but tonight, she let herself feel proud of how far she'd come. She grabbed her phone and quickly texted Miah and Freddie: Guess who's going to Tuskegee?

An exciting new chapter was taking off, like a plane taxiing down the runway, gathering speed for flight. And for the first time in a long time, Genesis felt like she wouldn't be soaring alone.

10

MENTOR MOTIVATION

A few weeks after the drone competition, Mr. Barlow surprised the trio with an unexpected trip. He didn't say much as he drove them out of the city, the familiar sounds of traffic fading into open skies and stretches of countryside.

When they finally pulled up to a small airfield, Freddie, Miah, and Genesis stared in awe at the rows of small planes lined up on the tarmac. The sunlight gleamed off the metal, and for a moment, it felt like stepping into a whole new world.

Freddie's heart raced as he took it all in, his excitement barely contained. "Yo, this is crazy!" he said, a grin spreading across his face.

"This is a little different from the flight school we visited back when you were all in eighth grade," Mr. Barlow said with a chuckle, leading them toward a hangar where a single plane sat parked outside.

The faint hum of an engine rumbled in the distance, blending with the crisp scent of jet fuel. Mr. Barlow pulled out his phone, capturing a quick picture as the trio slid on their sunglasses and struck playful poses in front of a plane, their laughter echoing across the open air.

Out of the hangar emerged a medium-sized, commanding figure in a flight suit. It was Lieutenant Colonel Michael Hales. His sharp posture exuded authority, but the warmth in his eyes and easy smile put them at ease immediately.

"Welcome to Willa Beatrice Brown Aviation. If you don't know her name, Google it!" He greeted them, his voice firm but inviting.

"I hear you all want to fly planes and have been making waves in the drone world." The trio exchanged nervous glances, unsure how to respond to someone who carried so much weight in the aviation world. Colonel Hales smiled, sensing their hesitation.

"Relax," he said, his tone reassuring. "We all start somewhere. Let me tell you my story." His voice grew steady, tinged with emotion as he recounted his journey. "I didn't come from much. My first flight was in a rickety old plane that sounded like it might fall apart in midair. But I wasn't gonna let that stop me. I had to work harder than anyone else, and I wasn't about to let anyone tell me what I could or couldn't do."

The trio listened intently, hanging on his every word. Freddie's nervous energy faded as he absorbed the Colonel's determination. Genesis leaned in, the story igniting a spark inside her. Miah stood with her hands in her pockets, her mind racing with possibilities.

Colonel Hales turned to Mr. Barlow, a smile breaking through his seriousness.

"And your instructor here is one of the best pilots I've ever flown with. He's told me about you all and how you're using drones to build a foundation to fly planes. That's a big deal. It means you've already got a head start on things like flight controls and spatial awareness, skills that'll carry over when you're in the cockpit of a real plane."

Freddie, Miah, and Genesis exchanged looks, their confidence growing under the Colonel's encouragement.

"Did I tell you," Mr. Barlow chimed in, grinning, "that they all passed the Part 107 exam last spring?"

Colonel Hales raised his eyebrows, clearly impressed. "That's no small feat. Drones are a real gateway into aviation," he said, nodding approvingly. "Your first FAA credential, how about that." He then shifted his focus to each of them, his expression curious. "So, what's the plan after high school? What kind of skies are you aiming for?"

Miah stepped forward first, her voice steady and filled with conviction. "I want to join the Air Force Academy, sir! My dream is to fly fighter jets."

The Colonel's eyes lit up. "The Academy is no joke, but if you're ready to work for it, they'll prepare you to be the best. You know about some of the women who've made it in the military as pilots, right? Like Swegle, Kimbrell, and Claiborne?"

Miah nodded eagerly. "Yes, sir. Their stories inspire me every day. I even have their posters on the ceiling in my bedroom so they're the first thing I see every morning."

Colonel Hales chuckled, clearly impressed. "*On the ceiling*, wow! That's the kind of focus it takes. Keep it up, and you'll be flying those jets sooner than you think."

Freddie was next, his voice carrying a mix of nerves and determination. "I'm thinkin' about flight school, sir. Still figuring out where, but I know this is what I want to do."

The Colonel gave a slow nod. "Flight school. Solid path. Lot of opportunity there. It'll give you the hands-on experience you need quickly.

If you're considering heading west, like Arizona, let me know. I've got connections that could help you get your foot in the door."

Finally, Genesis spoke, her voice quiet but resolute. "I want to go to Tuskegee University and study aviation science. For me, it's not just about flying, it's about being part of their legacy."

Colonel Hales' expression softened, a smile reaching his eyes, admiration clear. "Tuskegee is sacred ground in aviation, you know. You'd be standing on the shoulders of giants. And one day, someone else might say the same about you."

His words settled over them like a warm blanket, wrapping each of their dreams in a layer of validation and hope. For Miah, Freddie, and Genesis, this wasn't just a pep talk, it was a reminder that their dreams were possible, no matter how daunting the road ahead might seem.

As they headed back to the car, Colonel Hales handed each of them a business card. "Stay in touch," he said, looking at Miah in particular. "If you're serious about the military, I've got some people who can help guide you through the process. You might not need me, but you never know."

Miah took the card carefully, holding it like it was the key to her future. She glanced at Freddie and Genesis, and they all shared a quiet moment of understanding. Today wasn't just another day; it was a turning point.

On the drive back, the trio sat in thoughtful silence, each of them replaying the Colonel's words. Freddie looked out the window, imagining the cockpit of a plane with his hands on the controls. Genesis reread the Colonel's card, feeling the weight of Tuskegee's legacy settle over her shoulders like a cloak. Miah clutched the card in her hand, determination etched into her face.

For the first time, their dreams felt within reach. They weren't just kids with lofty goals anymore. They were future pilots, starting on a path to take on the skies.

11

RIVALS INVADE THE ZONE

Word spread fast after U-Street snagged fifth place, turning their once-overlooked drone club into a buzzing hub of energy. Freddie, Miah, and Genesis soaked in the newfound attention, but it wasn't long before that spotlight brought a new challenge, Riverside Academy.

Riverside wasn't just another team. They were *the* team. Their shiny new drones, top-tier gear, and smug attitudes screamed privilege. For U-Street, it wasn't just about drones anymore, it was about proving that grit could outshine gold.

One Friday afternoon, while the trio practiced in their makeshift parking lot "Drone Zone," Riverside decided to make their presence known. A crew of them rolled up, their uniforms crisp and their leader, Cameron, oozing smug confidence. Their drones gleamed under the sunlight, making U-Street's patched-up rigs look like toys by comparison.

Cameron strolled up, hands in the pockets of his hoodie, his grin on his face extremely annoying. "Well, well," he said, scanning the scene like he was judging a fashion show. "Practicing with these old things? Thought we'd stop by to see what we're up against."

Freddie's frown tightened as he stood his ground. "We use what we got. It ain't about what you fly, it's about how you fly 'em."

Cameron let out a sharp, cutting laugh. "Sure, keep telling yourself that, champ." He leaned in just enough to make it personal, his voice dipping into a smug whisper. "Remember that middle school championship baseball game?

Me, the unstoppable Cam-Man on the mound. Freddie, the so-called star at the plate. One swing. One miss. Game over."

He leaned back with a smug grin. "Face it, some things never change. Ask Big Rodney, he knew I was always better. That's why he quit. And it's only a matter of time before you and your little makeshift drone team quit too."

Freddie felt the jab like that fastball he whiffed on back then. The memory hit hard: his team counting on him, the star player, and yet, on that crucial day, his mighty swing cut through noting but air. He could still hear the disappointed whispers from the crowd in the stands, still see the frowns that mirrored his own.

His jaw clenched, and his frown deepened, but his gaze stayed firmly on Cameron. There was no way he was backing down. "That was then," he said, his voice steady and resolute. "This is now."

Miah wasn't about to let it slide. She stepped up, arms crossed, her smirk cutting through the tension. "Middle school? Seriously, *Cam-e-Boy*, is that what we doin'? This is a whole new competition, and trust me, we'll be ready. You should be worried about us."

Cameron's face twisted into a frown at Miah's words, but it didn't last long. With a quick shrug, his trademark smirk slid back into place. "Worried? Not even a little, U-Street." He glanced at his crew, signaling them to follow.

As they strode off, Cameron cast a smug glance over his shoulder. "Catch you at regionals, if you even make it."

Freddie exhaled sharply, trying to hold down the frustration boiling inside.

"Cameron thinks he can get in our head 'cause of some shiny drones and then come at me about a dumb baseball game back in middle school? That was five years ago." He swiped at his eyes, determined not to let the sting of tears show. "Cameron and his crew wanna roll up on our spot and talk crazy? We gon' show 'em what's up. We puttin' that bully on the bench for real. He ain't got no idea who he's messin' with."

Genesis stepped beside him, her gaze sharp as she watched Riverside disappear around the corner. "Now it's completely on," she said firmly, her voice low but laced with fire. "We're gonna put in the work on our end and crush those Busters next time we see 'em."

Freddie looked between Miah and Genesis, their faces reflecting the same determination he felt rising inside. His voice was steady now, filled with resolve. "Fifth place isn't good enough anymore. We're goin' for the win. Period!"

With that, the trio returned to their drones, the intensity of their practice hitting a new level. The hum of their patched-up rigs filled the parking lot, each maneuver sharper than the last. Every turn, every climb, and every descent was driven by the same purpose: To prove Riverside wrong.

As the sun dipped lower, painting the parking lot in warm orange hues, their drones zipped through the air with precision. This wasn't just practice anymore. Riverside wanted to talk trash and now, the gloves were off. And U-Street wasn't backing down.

12

PRESSURE

The rivalry with Riverside Academy had the squad on overdrive. Day after day, Freddie, Miah, and Genesis hit the dusty, cracked parking lot like it was their battlefield. The drones zipped and darted through cones, each maneuver sharper than the last. Miah focused on threading her drone through tight turns, her jaw clenched as she fought for precision.

Freddie pushed for speed, the hum of his drone cutting through the air as he shaved off seconds with every lap. Genesis was the brains behind it all, analyzing their every move, tweaking strategies until they felt rock-solid.

But as the competition loomed closer, the strain started to show. Exhaustion was written all over them, in the slump of their shoulders, the quiet grumbles when a drone clipped a cone, the heavy silence between practice runs. None of them said it out loud, but the pressure was hitting harder than Riverside had flexed. Each of them felt it, but Freddie? He was drowning!

The weight of his slipping calculus grade loomed over him like a storm cloud. Every failed test wasn't just a potential hit to his GPA, it was a potential blow to his father's backup plan in case his dream of becoming a pilot didn't pan out. Add the drones to the mix, and he felt like he was barely keeping his head above water. The two worlds collided, and Freddie was trapped in the middle.

One afternoon, after a particularly rough practice where his drone spiraled out of control twice, Freddie dropped to the ground, staring at the beat-up machine in his hands. His fingers traced a dented edge, frustration bubbling to the surface. The cheers and taunts from Riverside's crew earlier in the week still echoed in his mind, poking at his pride. "I'm never gonna get this," he muttered, his voice cracking. He leaned forward, pressing his hands to his face as the weight of everything came crashing down.

Miah noticed him first. She'd been resetting a cone, but when she saw Freddie slumped on the ground, her usual tough demeanor softened. She crouched beside him, her voice steady but gentle. "Freddie, you're thinkin' too much," she said. "We're good, we got this. You just gotta stop lettin' it get in your head."

Freddie shook his head, refusing to meet her eyes. "It's not just this, Miah," he said, his voice raw. "It's everything. I'm failin' calculus. And now I'm draggin' y'all down too." He quickly wiped at his face, hoping they didn't catch the tears threatening to spill.

Miah sighed, sitting fully on the pavement beside him, the orange glow of the setting sun painting the lot around them. "Freddie, stop," she said, her voice firm but kind. "You're not draggin' us down. We're all feelin' it, okay? But that's why we a team. We hold each other up when it gets rough."

Genesis joined them, kneeling on Freddie's other side. Her calm, steady presence broke through the tension like a cool breeze. "Still workin' with your calculus tutor?" she asked.

Freddie hesitated, his voice barely above a whisper. "I didn't get a tutor yet."

Miah's jaw dropped. Her sympathy vanished in an instant, replaced with exasperation. "Hold up, hold up! You mean to tell me you gettin' all this sympathy and never even got a tutor? What's wrong with you, bro?"

Freddie blinked, caught off guard by her sudden shift. "I... I don't know. I just didn't."

Miah pointed a finger at him, her tone sharp but playful. "Boy, don't let your momma find out, and please don't let her tell your daddy. I still remember what happened when you brought home that bad report card in middle school."

Freddie raised an eyebrow, already grinning despite himself. "Oh, here we go."

Miah smirked. "You made the mistake of tellin' everybody at school you were gonna be in trouble when your parents got home from work. So, of course, we all snuck onto the porch of your house, waitin' to see the show."

Freddie paused for a moment in surprise. "Wait, you mean my old house on 34th Street?"

"With the big front porch!" Miah replied with a grin. Genesis tilted her head, curious. "Wait, what happened?"

Miah threw up her hands, laughing. "Freddie was standin' in the livin' room lookin' real pitiful. Then suddenly his momma came into the room. She just looked at him at first and then she yelled at him so loud that the windows literally shook!

"All we heard was 'BaaBoom!' It sounded like thunder, and we thought a storm was about to start. All of us jumped up and took off running down the block like our lives depended on it. What made it even crazier was that the sun was shining, and the sky was completely clear, no clouds anywhere."

Freddie blinked, then burst into laughter. "Y'all did *what*?!"

"We got up outta there quick, you hear me!" Miah said, cracking up.

"Bro, please get a tutor. Don't have your momma pullin' up on drone practice, embarrassin' all of us."

Freddie laughed, but it was short-lived. He stared at his drone, then at his hands, now resting limply in his lap. "But what if I can't get my grade turned around?" he asked quietly. "What if I mess this up for all of us?"

Genesis exchanged a quick look with Miah, a silent agreement passing between them.

"Then we'll help you," Miah said, her voice leaving no room for argument. "You don't have to do this by yourself. We're a squad, Freddie. We got your back."

Genesis nodded, placing a hand on his shoulder. "She's right. Riverside's got fancy gear and big talk, but they don't have what we have. We'll beat them because of who we are, not what we've got. We need you on this team, bro."

Freddie took a shaky breath, their words slowly sinking in. For the first time in weeks, the storm in his chest began to quiet, even if just a little. "Alright," he said, his voice steadier now. "I'll look into gettin' a tutor. I'll fix this. For real this time."

Miah gave him a quick shove on the shoulder. "Good. 'Cause this ain't just about you, it's about all of us. The way they came at us, we gotta get 'em back."

As the trio sat on the pavement, the sky deepened into a rich purple, the air cooling around them. The hum of distant traffic and the occasional chirp of crickets filled the silence. The tension that had weighed so heavily on them earlier felt lighter now.

13

GENESIS' FIGHT

While Freddie struggled to pull up his grade, Genesis was fighting her own battle. A relentless nightly grind at the kitchen table.

After every drone practice, she'd come home, sit down, and dive into the endless stream of bookmarked websites, her laptop screen casting a pale glow across the dim room. No matter how many applications she submitted, there was always another hurdle to clear. Another essay to write. Another deadline lurking like a shadow. The pressure never let up, crushing her like a backpack overloaded with bricks she couldn't take off.

Her mom entered the kitchen, setting a steaming cup of tea on the table. She lingered for a moment, studying Genesis' tired eyes and the mess of papers spread out between them. "Any news yet?" she asked, her voice soft but edged with hope.

Genesis sighed, slumping in her chair. "Not yet. I've been gettin' emails sayin' I'm a finalist, but no real offers. "It's like I'm close enough to taste it, but I can't actually reach it." She shook her head, the knot of doubt twisting tighter in her chest. "What if I can't find any scholarships?"

Her mom reached out, squeezing her hand. "Listen, Genny, you've always been one of the most determined people I know. Something is going to happen. I believe that."

Genesis managed a small smile, but the words didn't quiet the storm raging inside her. After her mom left the room, the doubts crept back in, louder and meaner than ever. What if you can't get a scholarship? What if all this work is for nothing? What if Tuskegee slips through your fingers?

Her eyes fell on the Tuskegee acceptance letter sitting at the edge of the table. Seeing her name at the top should've been a comfort, a reminder of how far she'd come. But tonight, it felt like a taunt, a glimpse of a future that might not be hers. The weight of it pressed down on her, and she let her head fall into her hands, breathing through the wave of anxiety.

Hours passed. The kitchen grew quiet, the only sound was the soft hum of the refrigerator and the occasional clack of her keyboard. The streetlights outside cast long shadows across the table. Genesis stared at the letter again, her mind racing.

She thought about everything Tuskegee stood for, the history, the legacy, the giants who had walked its campus. She thought about everyone who believed in her: Her mom. Her friends. Her teachers, who said she had what it took. But the fear of falling short, of letting herself and everyone else down, gnawed at her.

The voices in her head whispered louder. Maybe you're not enough. Maybe you don't belong there.

Finally, she pushed back from the table, the chair scraping against the worn linoleum floor. Her eyes glanced at the clock. It was past midnight, but she didn't care. She stood for a moment, staring at the pile of applications. Then she whispered, "Not givin' up. No way."

With a deep breath, she grabbed her laptop, opened another application, and began typing. Her fingers flew across the keyboard, each keystroke carving out a space for her voice, her future. This wasn't just about Tuskegee anymore.

This was about proving something to herself. Proving she was worthy of this dream. Proving obstacle could stop her.

Echoes of a legacy.

The phrase lingered in her mind, more than just the title of her essay, it was a truth she was stepping into. The sacrifices of those before her, the battles fought, the doors cracked open just wide enough for her to push through. She wasn't just telling a story, she was stepping into one.

Exhaustion finally won. Genesis' head drooped, her fingers slipping from the keyboard as sleep pulled her under. She woke to the first rays of light spilling through the window, the soft glow casting long shadows over her scattered notes. The tea on the table sat cold and untouched, a forgotten casualty of her late-night grind. Rubbing the sleep from her eyes, she straightened up, resolve settling deep in her chest.

The echoes of a legacy reverberated through her, steady and insistent, a reminder that she wasn't just filling out applications.

She was building a future, one essay at a time.

14

IT'S ABOUT THE MONEY

As the regional drone competition crept closer, Mr. Barlow gathered the trio in the corner of the gym after practice. His expression was serious, the kind that made the air feel heavier. "Alright, team, we've got a problem," he began. "We need to raise money if we're going to keep competing. The equipment's falling apart, and travel expenses are stacking up. If we don't figure something out, this might be the end of the road."

Freddie frowned, the weight of the situation sinking in fast. "So what are we supposed to do? Sell cookies? Wash cars? Feels like we'd need a miracle."

Miah leaned against the wall, her brow furrowed in thought. "What about sponsorships?" she said, her voice steady with conviction. "There's gotta be some local businesses that'd back us. We can show them what we've done so far, our progress, our potential."

Genesis nodded, her mind already piecing together a plan. "And we can make a video. Show them who we are, what we're about. We could use clips from practice, the last competition, and even talk about what this team means to each of us."

Mr. Barlow's face broke into a grin, pride shining through his tired expression. "Now that's the kind of thinking I like to see. If we put together something solid, we might just get the support we need." And just like that, they were in motion.

Over the next week, the trio threw themselves into the project. Freddie took charge of editing, pouring hours into stitching together clips of their shaky starts, intense drills, and triumphant moments. As he worked late into the night, the frustration from his other struggles seemed to fade, replaced by a renewed connection to the team's story.

Meanwhile, Miah and Genesis hustled to compile a list of potential sponsors. They crafted emails, made phone calls, and brainstormed how to make their pitch as impactful as possible. Genesis, ever the strategist, kept everyone on track, while Miah's confidence pushed them to aim high.

When the video was done, it wasn't just a highlight reel. It was a story. It showed their gritty practices in the dusty parking lot, the pride on their faces when they placed fifth at the last competition, and heartfelt interviews from each of them. Genesis talked about her dream of attending Tuskegee University and how drones were her gateway into aviation. Freddie shared how the team gave him a purpose when he felt lost. Miah opened up about fighting to prove she could defy expectations and fly, no matter what anyone said.

The trio watched the final cut together, a quiet moment of pride passing between them. It wasn't perfect. But it was real. And it was them.

At first, the responses were slow. Days passed with little more than polite declines or complete silence, and the initial excitement started to wane.

Sitting in the cafeteria one afternoon, Freddie tapped his phone, refreshing their shared email inbox for the tenth time that hour.

"Maybe this was too much to hope for," he muttered, his voice tinged with doubt.

But just as Genesis was about to respond, Miah's eyes widened, and she leaned over her phone. "Wait, look! An email just came through from VertiSky STEM Solutions.

They wanna meet with us next week to talk about sponsorship!" Her voice rose with excitement, drawing the attention of a few nearby students.

Freddie's face lit up, his earlier doubt melting away. Genesis clapped her hands together, a grin spreading across her face. For the first time in weeks, the weight on their shoulders felt a little lighter.

"They're an aerospace company," Miah added, still reading the email. "If anyone would get why this matters, it's them." The trio exchanged glances, the nervous energy between them palpable. This wasn't just about getting some cash, it was about validation. They had put their hearts into sharing their story, and now someone was listening.

"We've gotta make this count," Freddie said, his voice steady with determination.

"And we will," Genesis replied firmly. "This is just the beginning."

As they left the cafeteria, their steps felt lighter, the weight of uncertainty replaced with a flicker of hope. There was still a lot to prove and even more to prepare for, but for the first time, it felt like they were moving toward something bigger.

15

MEETING VERTISKY

The day of the meeting with VertiSky STEM Solutions finally arrived. Freddie, Miah, Genesis, and Mr. Barlow stepped into the towering glass building, their excitement laced with nerves. The polished floors gleamed under bright lights, and the hum of productivity filled the air.

Everything about the place screamed success, making them feel like they'd stepped into a whole different world. They were greeted by Mrs. Irma Neal, VertiSky's CEO, a striking woman with sharp eyes that seemed to notice everything and a smile that immediately put them at ease. She extended a firm handshake to each of them, her presence commanding yet approachable. "So, you're the U-Street team I've been hearing about," she said, her tone warm but direct. "Your video was impressive. I could see the passion and grit behind your story, and that's something we value deeply here at VertiSky."

Freddie swallowed hard, feeling the weight of the moment. "Thank you, Mrs. Neal," he said, his voice steady but tight. "We've worked really hard to get where we are, but we're up against schools with way more resources. For us, it's not just about the gear, it's about proving that hard work and heart can compete with anything."

Mrs. Neal tilted her head slightly, considering his words. "I like that," she said, nodding.

"Passion is what drives innovation in this field. But I've seen too many people let obstacles stop them. What makes you different is your willingness to push through."

She paused, then smiled, her next words hitting like a thunderbolt. "VertiSky believes in investing in the next generation of aerospace leaders. That's why we're offering to sponsor your team. We'll cover your travel expenses for the upcoming competition and provide an upgrade to your equipment, including the latest first-person view technology."

The room went silent for a beat as her words sank in. Then Miah blurted out, "Wait, you're serious? You'd really do that for us?" Her wide eyes betrayed her disbelief.

Mrs. Neal's smile widened, her tone almost playful. "Absolutely. But," she added, leaning forward slightly, "there's a catch."

Freddie's stomach dropped, and the trio held their breath.

"You'll need to visit VertiSky a few afternoons before the competition," Mrs. Neal explained. "We'll introduce you to how our engineers work, the process of developing cutting-edge drones, and how this technology is shaping the future of aviation, including urban air mobility and vertiports. This isn't just about funding; it's about gaining insights that will make you smarter, sharper competitors. Trust me, it'll be worth your time."

Genesis couldn't hold back her grin. "Urban air mobility and vertiports, that's a whole new level. *We'd absolutely* love to be part of that," she said, her excitement clear in her voice. "Thank you so much for believing in us."

Mrs. Neal stood, shaking their hands once more. "Belief is earned, and you've done that. Now, show us what you can do with the right support."

As they left the building, the trio was buzzing with excitement. Out in the parking lot, they couldn't contain themselves. Miah threw an arm around Freddie's shoulder, laughing.

Genesis clapped her hands together, her face alight with joy. Even Mr. Barlow, usually calm and collected, was grinning ear to ear.

"Upgraded FPV, oh, this is huge," Miah said, her voice still tinged with disbelief. "We're not just gonna compete, we're gonna crush it."

Freddie nodded, but the hint of doubt that always lingered in his mind flickered. "Yeah," he said quietly, "but now we really gotta bring it. No excuses."

Genesis caught his eye, her voice firm but encouraging. "And we will. This isn't the end, it's just the beginning. We're gonna show VertiSky they made the right choice."

As they piled into Mr. Barlow's car, their chatter filled the air, the energy between them electric. VertiSky's sponsorship wasn't just a lifeline, it was proof that their dreams were valid.

16
PREP FOR REGIONALS

With VertiSky's sponsorship locked in, Freddie, Miah, and Genesis hit the ground running. Every afternoon after school, they were at VertiSky's sleek headquarters, soaking up knowledge from the engineers. The sessions were intense but electric. Learning to fine-tune their drones and master advanced flight techniques gave them a whole new edge. Still, the shadow of Riverside Academy loomed large. This wasn't just about winning; It was about proving they belonged.

Freddie thrived in the technical environment, his excitement evident as he tinkered with the upgraded drones. The engineers treated him like one of their own, and he couldn't get enough of the intricacies that made the new drones faster, smoother, and more agile. "This is what we needed," he said during a session, his eyes gleaming. "With these upgrades and the stuff we're learnin', we're gonna crush Riverside."

But even as the words left his mouth, a familiar doubt bubbled beneath the surface. Memories of striking out against Cameron in that middle school baseball game still haunted him. Freddie clenched his jaw, determined not to let the past repeat itself.

Miah was just as focused, though her mind was a storm of worries she refused to let show. As she guided her drone through intricate maneuvers, her father's voice echoed in her head: *"Flying jets is reckless, especially for a girl. Find something safer."* She gritted her teeth, shoving the thought aside. The pressure felt like a weight on her chest, but she was determined to carry it.

"We can't just rely on the new drones," she told Freddie, her voice steady but firm. "It's how we use them that matters. Mistakes will cost us, fancy gear or not."

Genesis was the team's strategist, always looking ahead. She poured over competition routes, sketching out the best approaches and analyzing how to save time on tricky turns. Late one evening, she sat with Mr. Barlow, pointing at a map of the course. "It's not just about being fast," she said, her tone measured. "We have to be precise. One bad turn could put us behind, and that's all Riverside would need to take the lead."

Despite her calm exterior, Genesis couldn't ignore the clock ticking in the back of her mind. Scholarship deadlines were approaching, and Tuskegee's tuition weighed heavily on her. She knew that winning could help ease that burden, but the stakes felt impossibly high.

Mr. Barlow kept a watchful eye on all three of them, stepping in when they needed encouragement. After a grueling practice, he gathered them around, his voice calm but firm. "You've all come so far," he said, looking at each of them. "Remember, this isn't about being perfect. It's about channeling the pressure to do your best. Trust yourselves, and trust each other." His words hit home.

For a moment, the tension seemed to lift, and the trio shared a quiet moment of understanding. They weren't just a team, they were family, holding each other up in ways no one else could.

As the regional competition drew closer, their training hit a new level of intensity. Late-night practices became the norm, the drone zone buzzing with the hum of motors and the occasional groan of frustration. Yet, amidst the exhaustion, a quiet confidence began to build. They weren't just fighting for a trophy. They were carrying the pride of U-Street High and their community on their shoulders.

One evening, as practice wrapped up under the dim glow of the parking lot lights, Freddie looked at Miah and Genesis. His voice was quiet but resolute. "We got this," he said, more to reassure himself than them.

Miah smirked, nudging his shoulder. "Facts!"

Genesis nodded, her eyes steady and focused. "No more doubts. We're ready!" They exchanged determined looks, the unspoken bond between them stronger than ever.

The regional competition wasn't just another event, it was their moment to prove that they weren't underdogs anymore.

17
REGIONAL COMPETITION DAY

The regional drone competition was alive with energy, a pulsing symphony of buzzing drones, excited chatter, and the occasional squeal of sneakers on polished floors. The massive gymnasium was packed with teams from across the state, each eager to prove their skill. Freddie, Miah, and Genesis stood together near their setup, taking it all in. The intensity of the moment made Freddie's heart pound so hard he could feel it in his ears.

Teams from prestigious schools moved with crisp efficiency, unpacking high-tech gear and calibrating their drones like seasoned pros. Across the way, Riverside Academy stood out, their team clad in matching uniforms, their drones sleek and customized to perfection. Cameron, their ever-smug leader, glanced over at U-Street with a smirk, making Freddie's jaw tighten. He couldn't let that get in his head.

Freddie glanced up at the massive scoreboard flashing the preliminary rankings. He wiped his damp palms on his jeans and muttered, "We got this," though his voice wavered slightly. The weight of the moment pressed on him harder than he'd expected.

Miah scanned the course, her lips pressed into a thin line. Her fingers tapped anxiously against the controller, the familiar knot in her stomach twisting tighter.

"This is... a lot," she admitted under her breath, her eyes darting over the complicated layout of the course. She adjusted her grip, grounding herself. We belong here, she reminded herself, though her hands trembled slightly.

Genesis stood still, her sharp eyes tracking Riverside's team as they ran final checks on their drones. Every movement was smooth, calculated, making U-Street feel like they were standing under a harsh spotlight, a silent reminder of who really controlled things at this competition.

Genesis swallowed hard, forcing herself to breathe evenly. *We've worked too hard to let this shake us*, she thought, brushing her sweaty palms against her jeans. She caught Freddie's eye and gave him a small nod, a silent message of solidarity. The announcer's voice crackled through the gym's PA system, calling U-Street to the field. Freddie's stomach lurched, but he forced his feet to move. As they stepped into the spotlight, the noise of the crowd swelled, and the buzz of drones overhead felt louder than ever.

Freddie stole a glance at Miah, who was gripping her controller so tightly that her knuckles were starting to go numb. Genesis stood calm but focused, her lips pressed together in a firm line as they all pulled their goggles over their eyes. They were all feeling it. The nerves. The pressure. The stakes. But this was what they'd worked for.

The buzzer sounded, and the drones shot into the air. Freddie's hands moved instinctively, guiding his drone through the first checkpoint. His heart raced in time with the drone's hum, but he forced himself to stay steady. Genesis' drone followed close behind, her movements precise as she navigated each obstacle. Miah brought up the rear, her drone wobbling slightly as she fought to steady her grip.

The tightest turn of the course loomed ahead. Miah's breath hitched as her hand slipped for just a second, her drone dipping dangerously low.

Panic flashed in her eyes, but she gritted her teeth and righted it just in time. *Stay focused*, she told herself, pushing the doubt away.

Freddie's fingers ached from the constant strain on the controls, but he kept his movements sharp, refusing to let fatigue win.

Genesis' sharp reflexes saved her from clipping a barrier, and she exhaled in relief, quickly refocusing on the next stretch. The three of them moved as a unit, their drones flying in sync as they neared the final leg of the course.

The finish line came into view, sending a surge of adrenaline through them. Freddie's drone shot across first, with Genesis and Miah close behind. As their drones came to a halt, the trio lifted their goggles and exhaled in unison, their chests rising and falling from the intensity of the race.

They huddled together, controllers still in hand, waiting for the scores. The noise of the gym faded into the background, replaced by the pounding of their hearts. For a moment, time seemed to stand still as they stared up at the scoreboard, hope and fear swirling inside them.

When the scores flashed across the screen, their eyes widened. U-Street High: Tied for Second Place after Round One.

Relief and pride washed over them like a wave. Genesis let out a breath she hadn't realized she'd been holding. Miah broke into a wide grin, nudging Freddie's shoulder. "Told you we belong here," she said, her voice full of fire.

Freddie smiled back, his earlier doubts melting away. "We're not done yet," he said, his voice steady. "Next round, we're taking first." They exchanged determined looks, the bond between them stronger than ever. This was their moment, and they were ready to rise to it.

18

SHOWTIME

The gym buzzed with nervous energy, so thick it felt almost tangible. The final round had arrived, and Freddie could feel the weight of it in his chest. His heart pounded as he stepped into position, gripping the controls like they were the only thing tethering him to the moment. The lights were brighter, the crowd louder, and the stakes higher than ever.

The buzzer sounded. Freddie's drone shot forward, slicing through the first set of obstacles with precision. His movements were sharp, his focus laser-tight. Behind him, Miah was locked in, her hands steady on the controls despite the tremor of nerves twisting in her stomach. Genesis, ever the strategist, called out quick adjustments, her voice slicing through the chaos.

"Tighter on that turn, Freddie. Miah, you're clear, keep pushing!" The trio moved in perfect sync, their drones weaving through tight turns and steep climbs as if they were extensions of their own bodies. The competition was fierce, but they were holding their own.

Then, disaster struck. Miah's drone wobbled mid-turn, veering off course, its altitude dropping fast. Her heart leapt into her throat.

"Freddie! My drone's goin' down!" she shouted, panic cracking her voice.

Freddie's pulse spiked, but he forced himself to stay calm. "Easy, Miah!" he called, his voice firm, steady. "Don't overcorrect. Pull up nice and slow, you got this."

The crowd collectively gasped as Miah's drone dipped dangerously low, its propellers sputtering under the strain. The sound sliced through the tension in the room. Every second felt like an eternity as she fought to stabilize it.

The drone shuddered, then steadied. Slowly, it rose, regaining control. The crowd erupted in cheers and sighs of relief, but Miah barely heard them. She forced herself to breathe, jaw tight, hands gripping the controls like a lifeline. "I'm good," she said, though her voice still shook. "Let's finish this."

Genesis' voice came sharp and clear. "We're still in it! Push hard on the final stretch, we can make up the time!" Freddie didn't need to be told twice. His hands moved instinctively, guiding his drone into the steep vertical climb ahead, the hardest part of the course, the section where every team struggled.

Elevation changes demand perfect control, especially sudden up-and-down moves. One wrong adjustment, and the drone could spiral out, lose momentum, or fail to recover before crashing. Freddie kept his line tight, urging his machine higher and faster.

Behind him, Miah pushed harder than ever, her earlier slip forgotten as she fought to stay on his tail. The climb was brutal, but she gritted her teeth and powered through, refusing to let doubt slow her down. Genesis followed close, her focus razor-sharp as she calculated their timing down to the second. The rapid altitude shifts tested every bit of their reflexes, but she trusted the work they'd put in. They weren't just racing. They were executing a plan. This was where teams fell apart. But not them.

The final stretch blurred past in a mix of speed and precision. The trio moved as one, their drones darting through the last obstacles with an electric combination of desperation and determination. The crowd roared as they crossed the finish line, the sound crashing over them like a wave.

Freddie's eyes shot to the scoreboard, his chest rising and falling as he tried to catch his breath. For a moment, everything seemed to hang in suspended silence.

Had they done enough? Had all the late nights, the sweat, the tears been worth it?

Then, the numbers lit up. U-Street High: First Place.

Freddie exhaled sharply, the weight of it hitting all at once. They had done it. By the slimmest margin, they had edged out Riverside, whose pilots had lost precious time miscalculating the elevation portion of the course.

Miah let out a breathless, disbelieving laugh, her hands still trembling on the controls. Genesis broke into a wide grin, her usual composure crumbling under the sheer thrill of victory.

Freddie looked at his team, his friends, and knew that this win wasn't just a trophy. It was proof. They had beaten the odds, silenced the doubters, and shown that grit and determination could stand up to privilege and resources. The three of them huddled together, their faces glowing with pride and relief. This wasn't just a victory. It was a statement.

19

SWEET VICTORY

When the trio stepped down from the awards podium, their hands still gripping the shiny first-place trophy, they spotted Cameron storming toward them. His usual cocky swagger was gone, replaced with stiff shoulders and a scowl that barely masked his frustration. "Don't think this means you're better than us," Cameron snapped, his tone sharp and dripping with bitterness. "Y'all just got lucky today."

Freddie raised an eyebrow, exchanging a quick glance with Miah and Genesis. His slow grin spread wider as he let the trophy gleam under the lights. "Lucky? Nah, Cam. That was skill," he said, his voice casual but loaded with satisfaction. "We earned this, homie."

Cameron's jaw clenched, his eyes darting between the trio and the trophy. "Whatever," he muttered, jamming his hands into his pockets. "Enjoy it while you can. We're takin' you down next time."

Miah stepped forward, her arms crossed, her smirk sharp. "Next time, huh? You better bring more than shiny drones and that trash you're talkin', 'cause we ain't goin' nowhere."

Genesis smirked, not bothering to hide her grin. "There's levels to this!" she said, her voice smooth but razor-sharp. "We can settle this right now. Or better yet, name the time and we'll come to your school's parking lot."

Cameron scoffed, his voice edged with irritation. "We don't fly our drones in a parking lot. We have a drone cage."

Freddie smirked, leaning in just enough to make his next words hit their mark. "Maybe it's time for you and your team to head back to *your* cage. Don't worry, we'll make sure you don't starve. We'll even toss you some scraps."

Cameron glared at them for a moment, then spun and walked off, his team trailing behind him in uncomfortable silence. Freddie let out a laugh as he turned back to his friends, the grin never leaving his face. "That was fun," he said, holding the trophy up. "Not just the win, but shuttin' that dude up. That's icin' on the cake."

Miah laughed, nudging him with her elbow. "Bro, you know he's gonna lose sleep over this one." Genesis adjusted her grip on the trophy, her smile softening. "Let him," she said after a pause. "We earned this. All of it."

Outside the gym, the late afternoon sun turned the trophy into a glowing beacon as they stepped into the cool air. Mr. Barlow was waiting for them by the entrance, his expression a mix of pride and emotion. "You three" he began, shaking his head like he couldn't believe it. "You've come so far. Today wasn't just about winning. It was about handling the pressure, overcoming setbacks, and sticking together. That's what matters most. That's what's going to carry you forward, not just here, but in everything you do."

Miah looked at her friends, her face softening as Mr. Barlow's words sank in. The trophy was amazing, but she knew he was right. This wasn't just about the win, it was about the journey they'd taken to get there. They'd fought their fears, leaned on each other, and proved they could stand shoulder to shoulder with the best.

Genesis held the trophy a little tighter, her voice quiet but steady. "We couldn't have done this without you, Mr. B. You believed in us even when we weren't sure we could do it ourselves."

Freddie gave a small nod, his usual bravado giving way to something more genuine. "Yeah, thanks for stickin' with us, Mr. B."

Mr. Barlow's smile widened, his eyes glinting with pride. "Always. Now go celebrate, you've earned it."

Miah's face lit up, the sparkle of excitement returning to her eyes. "Pizza. We're gettin' pizza. Non-negotiable."

Freddie laughed, slinging an arm around her shoulders. "Only if I pick the toppings. No crazy stuff."

Genesis rolled her eyes, but her grin slowly faded into a slight frown. "You pick pineapples, and I'm out."

Their laughter rang out into the fading afternoon as they headed to the pizza spot, three friends, one trophy, and a bond stronger than ever. The competition was over, but their journey had only just begun.

20

OPPORTUNITIES KNOCK

In the weeks after the regional competition, life changed for Freddie, Miah, and Genesis in ways they couldn't have imagined. Their victory didn't just earn them a trophy, it opened doors they never thought they'd walk through. VertiSky announced they'd extend their sponsorship for future competitions, giving U-Street's drone club the resources to dream bigger. Local media outlets started covering their story, calling them the "Underdogs of the Skies." What had once been an overlooked after-school club was now a team on the rise. But the recognition was just the beginning. Real, life-changing opportunities began to roll in.

For Miah, it came in the form of a crisp envelope delivered to her doorstep. Inside was a personal invitation from Colonel Hales himself: *A chance to visit an Air Force training base.* She stared at the letter, her heart pounding as she read the words aloud: *"Meet with top pilots and learn firsthand what it takes to fly fighter jets."* Miah's hands trembled, but her mind was steady. This was it. The step that will make her dreams feel real.

For Freddie, winning regionals ignited something deep inside him. The confidence he'd built on the drone field spilled over into his toughest battle yet, calculus. Determined not to let it stand in his way, he doubled down, attending tutoring sessions and grinding through late-night study sessions, tackling problems he once avoided.

Slowly but surely, the numbers started making sense. When he scored a C on his first quiz, it wasn't discouragement, it was proof that he was making progress. For the first time, flight school didn't feel like a distant dream. It felt possible.

Genesis had her turning point in the form of a late-night email. She stared   at her laptop screen, reading and rereading the words: *"Congratulations! You have been awarded a full scholarship to the Tuskegee University Aviation Science Program."* Her heart raced as the reality hit her. This wasn't just a step, it was a leap. She laughed, tears streaming down her face as she thought about all the late nights, All the doubts she'd pushed through. Tuskegee wasn't a dream anymore, it was her future.

That night, the trio found themselves back on the rooftop, their old sanctuary. The city stretched out before them, its lights twinkling against the endless expanse of sky. The air was cool, and the moment felt like it belonged only to them. For a while, they sat in silence, letting the weight of their journeys settle. Then Freddie spoke, his voice steady and full of hope. "You know… we've faced so much to get here. But what's wild is, this ain't the end. This is just the start."

Miah smirked, tilting her head toward him. "Yeah, and now that we know what we're capable of, there's no stoppin' us."

Genesis looked out at the horizon, her smile soft but resolute. "We're gonna fly," she said, her words carrying a quiet power. Freddie grinned, his voice firm with conviction. "Yeah, *we're gonna* fly."

The road ahead wouldn't be easy, but that didn't matter. They had already proven their strength. And as long as they faced the challenges together, they felt that nothing could stop them.

21

NEW CHALLENGE

The regional win had put U-Street's drone club on the map. Invitations to new competitions and events flooded in, and with them came a fresh set of challenges. Freddie, Miah, and Genesis found themselves stretched thin, trying to juggle school, drone practice, and their growing personal goals. The thrill of success was still fresh, but so was the weight of everything that came with it.

One afternoon, after an intense practice, Mr. Barlow called the trio over. He held up a glossy flyer, a grin tugging at the corners of his mouth. "I've got some news for you," he said, his voice buzzing with excitement. "There's a national drone competition next month in Philadelphia. This isn't just any event, *it's the big leagues*. Schools from all over the country will be there, and I think you're ready."

Miah's eyes widened, her competitive spirit sparking to life. "Nationals? Are you serious?" she asked, the words tumbling out before she could stop herself. "We have to do this!"

Mr. Barlow nodded but raised a hand. "Hold on, let me explain."

He glanced between them, his tone steady. "This competition isn't just about speed. It's a full test of skill and strategy.

First, you'll design and build a team drone. It'll be based on a pre-made model. Then you'll race it through a high-speed course.

Second, there's an aeronautical navigation challenge. You'll assemble a navigation kit and use it to map out specific airspace classes. Accuracy is everything.

And finally, the grand finale: an obstacle race with hidden twists designed to push your precision and teamwork to the limit."

He let the weight of it settle before adding, "And just so you know, it's all against the clock." His gaze locked onto each of them. "This is going to push you harder than anything you've done before." He paused, then asked, "So... what do you think?"

Freddie's stomach twisted. The idea was exciting, but it also felt overwhelming. He rubbed the back of his neck, his voice uncertain. "It sounds incredible, but... do we really have time for this? I'm barely keepin' my head above water with calculus."

"Did you finally see a tutor?" Genesis asked, arching an eyebrow. Freddie let out a sigh. "Yeah... I got a C on my last quiz, so I guess it's progress. But man, this stuff is still tough, it's like my brain refuses to cooperate."

Genesis folded her arms. "Schedule a meeting with Ms. Hill. I'm tellin' you, she's the best."

Freddie hesitated, then blurted out, "Alright, Ms. Hill, I'll schedule time. But seriously, do we even have time to get ready for a competition in Philly?

Miah's deep in her Air Force Academy prep, you're juggling everything for Tuskegee, and, oh yeah, graduation is basically right around the corner."

Genesis folded her arms, her brow creasing as she thought it over. "It's a lot," she admitted, her voice steady.

But we've always found a way to make things work. Nationals is a once-in-a-lifetime opportunity. How can we pass that up?"

Mr. Barlow studied their faces, easily catching the hesitation in their expressions. His voice softened. "Look, this is your call. I won't force it. But I will say this, I've seen what you three can do. I know you have what it takes. The question is... are you willing to commit?"

The trio fell silent, each of them grappling with the weight of the decision. Freddie's mind raced through all the late nights, the setbacks, the doubts they had pushed through just to get here. He exhaled sharply, his fists clenching as that familiar spark of determination ignited inside him. Then, he broke the silence. "I'm in," he said firmly.

"We've come this far, what's one more challenge?" A smirk spread across his face, his confidence growing. "Besides, I'm sure Riverside will be there... and we need to put them in their place again."

Miah nodded, her lips curling into a smirk. "You know I'm not about to back down now. But if we're doin' this, we gotta be smart. No more wingin' it. We need a plan and we stick to it."

Genesis gave a sharp nod, her resolve solidifying. "Then it's decided. We're goin' to Nationals. But like Miah said, we have to be ready. Not just good, great."

Mr. Barlow's grin widened, pride shining in his eyes. "That's the spirit I was hoping for. Now, let's get to work."

As they walked out of practice that evening, the gravity of their decision started to sink in. Nationals wasn't just another competition, it was the biggest challenge they'd ever faced. But as the sun dipped below the horizon, casting warm hues across the city, they felt the same fire that had carried them through before. There was no room for doubt now. The countdown had begun, and they were ready to face whatever came next. Together.

22

NUMBERS IN MOTION

Freddie hesitated for days before finally taking Genesis' advice. His calculus grade was stuck around the C range, and with Nationals coming up, he knew he couldn't afford to let it slip any further. So, he did something he never thought he'd do. He scheduled a tutoring session with Ms. Hill, hoping, maybe even praying, that she could make sense of the chaos in his head.

Now, sitting across from her in the Learning Center, he let out a sigh and dropped his notebook onto the table with a dull thud. His calculus textbook lay open, its pages crammed with symbols and equations that might as well have been written in another language.

"I swear, Ms. Hill, I'm just not built for this," he muttered, rubbing his temples. "All these limits, derivatives, integrals, it's like trying to fly a drone blindfolded."

Ms. Hill smiled knowingly, tapping her pencil against the table. "Funny you say that, Freddie."

She leaned forward, flipping to a blank page in his notebook. "Because calculus is a lot like drone racing."

Freddie raised an eyebrow. "How?"

Ms. Hill smirked. "Alright, tell me this, when you're racing, how do you know when to speed up or slow down?"

Freddie shrugged. "I don't know, I just feel it. Like, when I'm coming out of a turn, I know I have to hit the throttle or I'll lose momentum. And if there's a sharp drop, I can't just full-send it. I have to ease into it, or I'll lose control."

Ms. Hill grinned. "Exactly. That's calculus."

Freddie blinked. "Wait...what?"

She picked up her pen and sketched a simple slope. "Imagine you're riding a bike down hill. The steeper the hill, the faster you go, right?"

"Yeah," Freddie said cautiously.

Ms. Hill nodded. "That steepness? That's a derivative, it tells you how fast your speed is changing. In drone racing, if you know how steep a climb or drop is, you can predict how much you need to adjust your throttle. If you don't, you either lose too much speed or crash because you're going too fast."

Freddie sat up a little. "So, wait... derivatives are like figuring out when to push my drone and when to ease up?"

Ms. Hill laughed. "Bingo."

She flipped to another page and drew a zigzag line. "Now, let's talk about optimization. Imagine an obstacle course. You want to find the best path through it without wasting time, right?"

"Of course," Freddie said. "If I take wide turns, I lose speed. But if I cut them too sharp, I could spin out or stall."

"Exactly," Ms. Hill said. "Calculus helps you find the perfect balance, just like when you're flying. It's all about finding the most efficient way to get from point A to point B."

Freddie leaned in, nodding slowly. "That actually makes sense…"

Ms. Hill wasn't done. "Now, what happens if a drone makes a sharp stop instead of a smooth turn?"

"It slows down too much," Freddie answered automatically. "You wanna keep a smooth curve so you don't kill your momentum."

"Smooth curves, that's calculus, too," Ms. Hill said with a smile. "Derivatives and integrals help figure out how to transition between speeds without abrupt changes. If your drone moves too suddenly, it's like taking a sharp turn instead of easing into it. But if you plan your movement, you maintain speed."

Freddie exhaled, staring down at the notebook. "Wait… so all these equations, all these graphs, they're basically just telling me how things change over time, like how my drone moves?"

Ms. Hill nodded. "Exactly. Once you understand that, you can predict where your drone will be before it even gets there. That's why calculus matters. It's not just numbers, it's about motion, control, and precision. Just like in a race."

Freddie looked at the page, then at his drone sitting beside him on the table. It clicked.

All those frustrating formulas, all those weird symbols, they weren't just random rules. They were the math behind: The way his drone flew. The way he adjusted in mid-air. The way he calculated every turn without even realizing it.

He looked up at Ms. Hill, a slow grin spreading across his face. "So… calculus is basically just drone racing in numbers?"

Ms. Hill laughed. "I'd say that's a fair way to put it."

Freddie picked up his pencil, a newfound understanding washing over him. "Now I get why my father wanted me to take calculus, it all makes sense now," he said. For the first time, calculus didn't feel impossible. It felt like flying.

Smirking, he flipped the page in his notebook. "Ms. Hill, you're a miracle worker! Now I can't wait for Nationals!"

23

THE BIG PUSH

Deciding to take on Nationals brought a whole new level of intensity to U-Street's drone team. With VertiSky's sponsorship covering travel and providing top-tier equipment, the stakes had never been higher. Their sleek new drones were faster, sharper and undeniably elite.

But they also carried an unspoken weight. Freddie felt it pressing squarely on his shoulders.

Every mistake felt like proof they weren't ready. That he wasn't ready. And if they failed at Nationals, it wouldn't just be a loss, it would be confirmation that U-Street didn't belong. So, he pushed.

Freddie threw himself into practice with relentless focus, leading the team through long, grueling sessions that stretched late into the evening. Every maneuver, every turn, every landing had to be perfect. "We're not just competing with locals anymore," he reminded them, his voice sharp over the hum of the drones. "This is the best in the country. We need to be flawless."

But as the weeks wore on, the pressure started to take its toll. Miah's focus wavered, her exhaustion deepening from endless late-night study sessions for her Air Force Academy prep.

Genesis, usually the steady one, struggled to juggle Tuskegee's class registration, orientation deadlines, and practice. The weight of it all chipping away at her usual calm.

Even Freddie, who prided himself on pushing through anything, felt his frustration spike when a maneuver didn't go as planned. His patience wore thin with every misstep.

One evening, after yet another punishing practice, the gym lights flickered overhead as they packed up their gear. Miah set down her controller with a sigh, her voice cutting through the silence. "Freddie, we need to talk." She crossed her arms, frustration clear in her stance. "You're pushin' too hard. I get it. We want to win. But we're not machines. I'm barely keepin' up with school, and I know you're feelin' it too."

Freddie wiped sweat from his face, his jaw tightening. His mind was still replaying the day's mistakes, obsessing over how to fix them. "Nationals won't wait for us to get it together," he shot back, frustration laced in his voice. "If we don't push now, we'll regret it later."

Genesis, ever the strategist, stepped in before the tension could climb any higher. Her voice was calm but firm. "Miah's right. We're all feeling the strain, Freddie. If we keep this up, we'll burn out before we even get to Nationals. Think about how we started, how many crashes we had. We didn't get better by overworking ourselves. We got better by trusting each other and working smart."

Freddie took a deep breath, her words sinking in. He had been so focused on proving they could compete at Nationals, proving that they belonged, that he hadn't realized how much it was draining them. "I just..." His voice softened. "I want us to show everyone what we're made of. To prove we belong. It feels like this is our last big shot, and I don't wanna mess things up."

Miah unfolded her arms, her stance loosening slightly. "Freddie, we're gonna win. I feel it. But we gotta do it right and together. No more burnin' ourselves out just to prove a point. We know who we are, and that's what matters."

Genesis nodded. "We'll rework the schedule. Make time for school, for practice, and for rest. That way, when Nationals hit, our minds and bodies will be ready."

Reluctantly, Freddie agreed, though frustration still simmered beneath the surface.

They spent the next hour reworking their training plan, adjusting schedules, setting limits, and finding a balance between pushing their limits and knowing when to step back.

It wasn't easy.

Miah sighed. "With this new plan, I'm not sure we'll have enough time to be at our best. And if that's the case, what's the point of even going?" Genesis shook her head, her voice firm but calm. "We will be at our best. But if we push too hard, we won't even make it to Nationals in one piece."

She picked up a marker and sketched a simple battery icon on the whiteboard. "Think of it like a drone race. If you overheat the battery, what happens?"

Freddie exhaled sharply, finally looking up. "You lose power before you reach the finish line."

Genesis nodded. "Exactly."

A tense silence settled over them, exhaustion hanging in the air like a thick fog. But then, something shifted. The tension loosened. The plan started coming together. As they stepped out of the gym that evening, the air was cool and still. Freddie looked up at the night sky, where stars began to peek through the fading twilight. They were small, distant specks but steady.

A reminder of everything ahead. Everything they had worked for. "Alright," he said quietly, his voice carrying a newfound calm. "Let's move smart, not just go hard. We got this on lock."

Miah and Genesis exchanged a look. They weren't completely convinced, not yet. But after weeks of stress, doubt, and exhaustion, something finally felt different. They still had a long road ahead. Nationals were looming. But for the first time in weeks, it felt like they were ready to face the challenge. Together.

24

THE NATIONAL STAGE

The moment they had been grinding for had finally arrived.

Genesis, Freddie, Miah, and Mr. Barlow stepped out of the van into the crisp Philadelphia air. A massive arena loomed ahead, its steel and glass exterior gleaming under the morning sun. For a moment, no one spoke. They just stood there, staring, absorbing the sheer weight of what lay ahead. This wasn't just any competition. This was *the* competition.

Inside, the air buzzed with an energy that crackled like electricity. Teams from across the country filled the venue, their voices blending into a chaotic symphony of excitement and nerves. The steady hum of practice drones zipped overhead, interrupted by bursts of applause as pilots executed flawless maneuvers.

Miah took a slow step forward, her fingers tightening around the strap of her backpack. Her eyes scanned the crowd, widening slightly at the sight of teams dressed in crisp, embroidered uniforms, their drones gleaming like futuristic masterpieces.

"Yo…" she muttered. This place is like the Drone Olympics, for real. One of their drones could fund our whole STEM program, maybe even fix the leaky roof in our cafeteria."

Freddie let out a slow exhale, shifting his gear bag over his shoulder. He could feel it, the weight of expectation pressing against his ribs, the familiar gnaw of self-doubt creeping at the edges of his thoughts. But he crushed it before it could take hold.

"Doesn't matter what they got," he said, his voice firmer than he felt. "We put in too much work to let this place get in our heads. We belong here."

Genesis nodded, rolling her shoulders back, forcing her body to relax. "Bigger stage, higher stakes, but the competition hasn't changed," she said, her voice even. "We fly the way we always do, smart, sharp, together."

Freddie and Miah exchanged a glance, then nodded. No more nerves. No second-guessing. It was time to fly.

The first event was a test of speed, precision, and teamwork: the Drone Build Race. Each team was given the same kit, a fully disassembled drone that included a frame, motors, propellers, a battery, flight controller and propeller guards. The goal? Assemble it, calibrate it, and fly it 90 feet to the finish line. Simple in theory. Brutal in execution.

The referee's voice boomed over the loudspeakers. *"Teams, take your mark... set... GO!"*

The room exploded into motion. Boxes ripped open. Parts scattered across tables. Hands flew in every direction as teams scrambled to assemble their drones at breakneck speed.

Freddie and Miah moved with the kind of synchronized precision that only came from years of practice. "Motor secured!" Freddie muttered, his fingers flying as he snapped wires into place, ignoring the sweat slicking his palms.

Miah caught the frame mid-air as Freddie tossed it, snapping the propeller and propeller guards into place with a sharp click. "Battery locked in!" she confirmed.

Genesis dropped to her knees, fingers hovering over the calibration buttons. Around her, the chaos swelled, shouts from other teams, the high-pitched whine of spinning motors, tools clanking against tables. But she tuned it all out.

"One second. Two. Come on...," she whispered.

The controller's light blinked green.

"We're live!" she announced. Freddie and Miah barely had time to exchange a breath before Genesis launched the drone into the air. It darted forward like a laser beam slicing through space in a blur of black and silver. Other teams were still struggling to stabilize their launches.

Genesis was already flying to win. She locked in, gripping the controller with steady hands, eyes locked on the finish line. The drone zipped past the halfway mark. A competitor's drone veered too hard and crashed. Another stalled mid-air. But U-Street's drone? Smooth. Fast. Unstoppable. Then, it crossed the finish line.

A split-second of silence. Then a burst of cheers as U-Street secured first place in the opening event. Freddie and Miah yelled, slamming into a victorious hug.

Genesis let out a slow, satisfied breath, her gaze flicking to the leaderboard: U-Street. Number one.

Mr. Barlow clapped a hand on Freddie's shoulder and high-fived Miah. "Now that's how you make an entrance. One event down, let's keep the pressure on."

As they looked around the buzzing arena, something shifted. This wasn't just a competition anymore. This was *their* competition. U-Street hadn't come all this way just to compete. They were here to win.

25

FRACTURED FLIGHT

The second event, the Aeronautical Navigation Challenge, brought a new intensity, the air inside the arena felt heavier than before. Each team had to assemble a navigation kit, plot airspace classes from A through D, and mark coordinates on PVC pipes representing latitude and longitude.

This wasn't just about skill. It was about precision, patience, and nerves. U-Street was ready. Or so they thought.

Miah stood at the controls, selected as the pilot, while Freddie and Genesis worked quickly to assemble the kit. Freddie took charge of the calculations, his newfound confidence in calculus pushing him to double-check every detail. His brow furrowed in concentration, scanning the numbers with sharp precision.

Genesis focused on assembly, snapping components into place with practiced ease.

Then, the tension crept in. "Genesis, that piece goes here." Freddie pointed to a connector she had just placed.

"I know." Genesis' voice was tight as she shifted it slightly. "I got it!"

Freddie exhaled sharply, his patience wearing thin. "Well, double-check it, okay? We can't afford mistakes."

Genesis muttered under her breath but adjusted the piece. The tension simmered, unspoken but thick.

Miah glanced back, gripping the controller tighter. "Can you two chill? We got this. Focus." Genesis and Freddie exchanged a glare but fell silent. After forty-two minutes, they completed the navigation kit build.

Now, it was Miah's turn. She launched the drone smoothly into Class A airspace. The crowd murmured as the drone glided through the labeled ring, earning a solid round of applause. Her descent into Class B was just as controlled, drawing cheers from a few spectators. "You're killin' it, Miah!" Freddie grinned, a flicker of excitement breaking through the tension.

Genesis, still clipped in tone, nodded. "Keep it steady. Don't rush." Miah rolled her eyes but locked in, guiding the drone into Class C with perfect precision. Another clean maneuver. Confidence surged through them. They were almost there.

Then, it happened.

Miah lined up for the descent into Class D, her palms sweating. The finish line was right there. But her fingers ached from gripping the controls too tight. She exhaled sharply, trying to steady herself. Then, her grip slipped. The drone wobbled mid-air. Miah's fingers scrambled to recover.

A sharp crack. The propeller guard clipped the edge of the airspace boundary. And in an instant, the drone spiraled out of control.

"Miah!" Freddie's voice cut through the gasps from the crowd.

The drone hit the ground with a sickening thud. Silence. The weight of the crash settled over the team like a thick fog. Miah froze, staring at the broken drone pieces scattered across the floor. "I... I messed up," she whispered, her voice barely audible.

Freddie's frustration boiled over. "What happened, Miah? We were so close! You just had to hold it steady!"

Miah's head snapped up, her voice rising. "Oh, so now it's all on me? Maybe if you two weren't snappin' at each other while I was tryin' to focus, this wouldn't have happened!"

Genesis stepped forward, her tone sharp. "Don't put this on us. You were the pilot, it was your job to land it. We've been carrying this team just as much as you, and we didn't crash."

Miah's eyes flashed. Her fists clenched at her sides. "Carrying? You think you're carrying me? I've been putting in just as much work as both of you, if not more."

Freddie threw his hands up. "Enough! Arguing ain't gonna fix the drone! We're already behind, and if we don't pull it together, this whole thing is over."

The tension hung in the air like a storm about to break.

Genesis clenched her jaw but turned away, gathering the scattered drone pieces with tight, deliberate movements. Miah's hands trembled as she picked up the propeller guard, frustration boiling into tears she refused to let fall.

Freddie knelt beside Genesis, his voice softer now, but still tense. "We need to fix this. Now." They worked in strained silence, their movements quick but heavy with unspoken resentment.

By the time the drone was operational again, the other teams had already finished. U-Street completed the event, but their time placed them fifteenth, a crushing blow.

As they left the arena for lunch, the air between them was thick with tension. Miah walked ahead, her shoulders hunched, frustration radiating from every step. Genesis stayed close to Freddie, her jaw tight. "We can't afford mistakes like that again."

Freddie glanced at her but didn't respond. Because he knew she was right. But the bitterness between them felt like another obstacle they couldn't afford. Nationals weren't just testing their skills. They were testing their team. And right now, that team was starting to crack.

26

THE DECIDER

The final round loomed, and the air inside the arena pulsed with anticipation. The course ahead was brutal. Tight turns. Steep climbs. Narrow tunnels. Each designed to push teams to their absolute limits.

Freddie, Miah, and Genesis stood at the starting line, their drones powered up, goggles clutched in their hands. The weight of earlier mistakes clung to them like a shadow.

On either side stood the best of the best. To the right, Riverside Academy, their lead pilot Cameron flanked by teammates Omar and Lisa. To their left, Alabama Aerospace & Aviation High with Naomi, a rising star in the drone racing world, leading alongside her team members, Devon and Brianna.

As they pulled their goggles over their eyes, the world around them disappeared.

Now, it was just them and the drone's view, a dizzying perspective of towering obstacles, razor-thin gaps, and the finish line that felt miles away.

Mr. Barlow stepped forward, his voice cutting through their nerves.

"This is it," he said, his gaze steady. "You've faced challenges before and come out stronger.

Don't let anything pull you apart now. You're a team, always remember that."

Freddie nodded, inhaling deeply, though his chest still felt tight. Miah adjusted her controller, her jaw clenched, flashes of her last crash replaying in her head through the drone's eye. Genesis stayed quiet, hands steady on the controls, but the tension in her stiff shoulders spoke louder than words.

Naomi stood a few feet away, adjusting her shirt sleeves, her eyes locked on the track. She wasn't just here to compete; she was here to win.

The start signals blared, and the race began. Freddie's drone shot forward, slicing through the air with sharp precision. His FPV feed displayed every turn with crystal clarity, his mind razor-sharp as he tackled the first set of tight corners.

Miah followed close behind, her movements smooth but cautious, her field of view locked into the dizzying aerial perspective. Genesis brought up the rear, her eyes darting between the drones on her screen, calculating every fraction of a second.

The other teams mirrored their formation, Cameron leading for Riverside Academy, Naomi at the front for Alabama Aerospace & Aviation High, their teammates holding steady behind them, ready to capitalize on any mistake. The first obstacle was cleanly executed, but then, the climb loomed ahead. A steep, grueling ascent designed to test every pilot's nerve and precision.

Freddie neared the base of the climb, his drone's camera tilting upward, revealing the full height of the challenge. "Let's push it!" he called, urgency laced in his voice. Miah gritted her teeth, accelerating to keep up. Genesis followed, but the tension between them crackled like static in the air.

To their left, Naomi shouted something into her mic, and Devon surged forward, trying to overtake Miah before the climb. To their right, Lisa from Riverside Academy moved ahead of Genesis, attempting to block her from gaining speed.

It was more than just a race; it was a battle for positioning. The climb was brutal. Every inch upward demanded full control. Then, Miah's drone wobbled on her FPV screen. Her grip tightened, her breath shallow. Doubt clawed at her focus, the ghost of her last mistake haunting her. "I can't!" Her voice shook as the words broke free.

Freddie's voice cut through the comms like a blade. "You can, Miah. Pull it together. We need you."

She froze for a brief second, fingers trembling. Then, Genesis' voice. Steady. Certain. "Miah, we're in this together. Focus. We got your back."

Something clicked.

Miah exhaled, steadying her grip. The feed steadied. She guided her drone upward with renewed precision, shaking off the doubt. The trio crested the climb in unison, their drones moving like a synchronized flight team, tethered not just by skill, but by trust.

Naomi's Alabama Aerospace & Aviation High drone surged ahead, executing a flawless maneuver that left the crowd gasping. Omar from Riverside Academy edged closer to Freddie's drone, attempting to force him into a tighter angle at the next checkpoint. It was now a three-way race.

The last obstacle loomed ahead. A narrow, twisting tunnel barely wide enough for a single drone. Miah's FPV feed flickered, displaying the tight, spiraling walls ahead. The crowd roared as U-Street, Riverside, and Alabama Aerospace & Aviation raced neck and neck.

Freddie's drone entered first, the rapid buzz of propellers nearly drowned out by the pounding of his heartbeat. Naomi squeezed into the tunnel a split second later, her drone tilting at an impossible angle to maintain speed. Cameron stayed right behind her, using Riverside's signature precision to stay clean through the tunnel. Miah followed, her movements fluid, controlled, no hesitation this time. Genesis brought up the rear, her FPV view locked on the tiny space ahead, adjusting her angle by mere centimeters to avoid clipping the walls.

Then they emerged. The finish line was in sight.

Cameron's drone from Riverside Academy was inches ahead. Naomi from Alabama Aerospace & Aviation High refused to back down, pressing forward with relentless speed. Freddie pushed his drone to its limit, his goggles flashing warning signs of max speed. Miah and Genesis surged alongside him, each calculating their final moves with precision, clarity, and absolute control.

The drones crossed the finish line, and the arena erupted in cheers. But the scoreboard remained blank. U-Street huddled together, their breaths heavy, chests rising and falling in sync.

For the first time in a long time, the silence between them wasn't tense, it was filled with shared hope.

Then, the numbers flashed. 1st Place: Riverside Academy, 2nd Place: Alabama Aerospace & Aviation High, 3rd Place: U-Street High. The entire arena seemed to hold its breath for a beat. The sting of coming in third settled over them. But as their eyes met, something shifted. The tension that had held them together through the competition finally eased. In its place came something deeper. Understanding. Pride.

Genesis was the first to break the silence, her voice steady, carrying the weight of everything they had fought for. "We did that. Together."

Freddie let out a long breath, a small grin tugging at the corner of his lips. "Third place at Nationals. Against teams with way more resources? That's somethin' to be proud of."

Miah exhaled, only now realizing how tightly she had been holding onto the moment. Her voice was lighter, freer. "Yeah, it is." Then, a smirk.

"I don't know about you two, but that was way too much excitement for me," Freddie said, shaking his head dramatically. Laughter burst from all three of them, the weight of the past slipping away in the sound. They weren't just teammates anymore. They were family.

And though their high school drone racing journey had come to an end, the lessons learned, the battles fought, and the bond they built in the air? That would stay with them forever.

27

A DIFFERENT KIND OF VICTORY

As the trio stood on the podium, the third-place trophy gleaming under the bright lights, a flood of emotions surged through them. The weight of everything they had fought through felt heavier than the trophy in their hands.

They hadn't taken first. But this was never just about winning. It was about proving they could rise together even when everything seemed to fall apart. Applause thundered around them, but their focus remained on each other. Their unspoken bond, tested, fractured, and rebuilt, held them steady.

Miah nudged Freddie lightly, a small smirk playing on her lips. Genesis met his gaze, offering a quiet, knowing smile.

We did this together.

After the awards ceremony, Freddie spotted Cameron weaving through the crowd, making his way toward them.

He braced himself for some kind of smug remark, but Cameron's expression wasn't cocky this time. It was... different. Respectful, even.

Cameron extended his hand. "You guys really brought it today," he said sincerely. "That was some comeback. After the second round, I didn't think you'd recover like that."

Freddie hesitated for a split second before clasping Cameron's hand in a firm shake. "Yeah, well, we don't quit that easy," he said, his voice steady with pride. "But congrats. Y'all earned it."

Cameron nodded, his eyes shifting from his first-place trophy back to Freddie. "You know, I used to think winning was the only thing that mattered. But watching you guys fight through today... it made me rethink that. It's not just about the trophy, it's about the challenge. You pushed us, and honestly, that made this win mean more."

Freddie's brows lifted slightly. He hadn't expected that level of honesty from Cameron. "If I'm bein' real," Freddie admitted, "competin' with you always pushed me, too. Every time we went head-to-head, it forced me to level up. I wanted to beat you, but today... I'm just glad we were both here."

Cameron smirked, a flicker of his usual confidence returning. "Well, don't get too comfortable. Next time, it won't be that close."

Freddie chuckled, the tension between them shifting into something lighter. "Oh, I agree, it won't be close at all. We're crushin' you."

As Cameron turned to leave, Miah called out, "Hey, Cameron!"

He paused, glancing over his shoulder. "Yeah?"

Miah's grin was teasing. "Sorry for that *'Cam-e-Boy'* dig."

Cameron's smirk widened, unfazed. "It's all good, Miah. Maybe I should get your number so we can keep in touch?"

Miah raised an eyebrow, her smirk never fading. "Hit me up on IG."

Cameron chuckled, shaking his head as he backed away. "Alright, IG it is, just don't leave me on *read*, **though."**

Miah laughed softly, shaking her head as Cameron disappeared into the crowd. Freddie folded his arms, eyeing her with exaggerated judgment. "Well, well, look at you, team Cameron now, huh? G, you see this?"

Genesis smirked, nudging Freddie with her elbow. "She rollin' with the ops now."

Miah rolled her eyes, though she couldn't hide the smile creeping across her face. "What?! He's cute though."

The trio burst into laughter, the tension from earlier fading away. As they stepped away from the crowd, the moment finally caught up with them. The cheers, the trophy, the exhaustion, it all settled between them.

Genesis took a deep breath and spoke first. "Listen... about earlier. The arguing, the way we went at each other, I shouldn't have said what I did."

Miah exhaled, rubbing the back of her neck. "Yeah. Same. I was frustrated, but that wasn't on y'all. It was just... everything."

Freddie glanced at them both, then let out a small chuckle. "Guess we all had our moments, huh?"

Genesis nodded. "Yeah. But we still made it through. And if we ever do anything like this again, next time... we keep the fights to a minimum."

Miah smirked. "So, like, only one or two fights maybe?"

Freddie grinned, shaking his head. "You know what I mean." No dramatic apologies were needed. This was family. Tension, quarreling, pushing each other to the edge, but always coming back together in the end.

That's what family does.

Before they could continue, Mr. Barlow joined them, his pride evident as he draped an arm around each of their shoulders. "You three," he began, "you've shown the world what U-Street is all about. This isn't just about drones or trophies, it's about grit, teamwork, and heart. You've put this program on the map, and I couldn't be prouder."

They stood there, a small team with a big impact, soaking in the moment.

Miah grinned. "Don't get too sentimental on us, Mr. B. Just 'cause we're graduating doesn't mean next year's team can't take first. We kinda set the bar high, didn't we?"

Genesis nodded, her voice steady. "We laid the foundation. Now it's up to the next team to build on it."

Freddie's gaze shifted between them, the weight of their shared journey settling into something lighter, something hopeful. "This ain't the end for U-Street," he said quietly but with conviction. "Next time a U-Street team gets here, they're winnin'!"

As they left the arena, the late evening air wrapped around them, cool and refreshing after the heat of competition. They walked side by side, their bond stronger than ever. This victory wasn't just about third place or a trophy. It was about realizing that together, they could face anything. They had stumbled, fought, and risen again, not as individuals, but as a team.

28

RETURNING TO THE "U"

When Freddie, Miah, and Genesis stepped back into the U-Street High School building, they were met with cheers, high-fives, and an energy they'd never experienced before. Though they had placed third at nationals, the entire school celebrated them as champions. The once-quiet drone club had become the pride of U-Street, and their accomplishment rippled beyond the halls into the surrounding community.

A week after their return, Mr. Barlow organized a special assembly in the gym. The space buzzed with excitement as students and teachers packed the bleachers. Freddie shifted nervously as they stood on stage, but Miah nudged him playfully. "Relax," she whispered, "you're kinda famous now."

Mr. Barlow took the mic, his voice booming with pride. "Today, we celebrate three remarkable students who have shown us what determination, teamwork, and resilience can achieve. Freddie, Miah, and Genesis didn't just represent U-Street, they inspired us. They showed us that with grit and heart, anything is possible."

The crowd erupted into cheers, their energy filling the gym. Freddie glanced at Miah and Genesis, his chest swelling with pride. This moment wasn't just about them; it was about everyone who had supported them along the way.

After the applause died down, the trio stepped off the stage. A group of younger students swarmed them, their faces glowing with excitement.

"How do we join the drone club?" a wide-eyed boy asked, practically bouncing on his toes. Miah knelt to his level, her voice warm. "Just show up," she said with a smile. "Mr. Barlow's got all the tools to teach you, and he'll make sure you know everything we do."

Freddie watched the interaction, his heart full. These kids didn't just see them as competitors; they saw them as role models. He remembered what it felt like to be underestimated, and now, standing here, he realized they were helping to rewrite that narrative for everyone coming after them.

Mr. Barlow approached the trio, his eyes glinting with pride. "You've done more than win trophies," he said, his tone quieter now. "You've lit a spark. This school sees itself differently because of you three."

Genesis crossed her arms, a confident grin spreading across her face. "This is just the start, Mr. B. We'll keep comin' back to mentor. The U-Street Drone Team's only goin' up from here."

Miah chimed in, her tone light but sincere. "First place is comin' next. The team's already got a legacy, and it's only gonna grow stronger."

Freddie nodded, his voice steady. "We'll keep pushin'. U-Street's just gettin' started."

As they walked through the halls afterward, surrounded by eager classmates and younger students asking endless questions, the trio exchanged glances. The weight of their journey, the struggles, and even the moments of doubt now felt like steppingstones to something bigger. Their legacy wasn't just about winning. It was about opening doors, showing what was possible, and inspiring the next generation to aim higher.

29
THE NEXT EPISODE

The final two months of high school sped by in a blur of celebrations, good-byes, and preparations. Freddie, Miah, and Genesis stood at the edge of new beginnings, their paths diverging yet bound by the bond they'd forged through triumphs and trials. Graduation had come and gone, and now it was time to take Flight, literally and figuratively.

Miah was days away from heading to basic cadet training at the Air Force Academy in Colorado Springs, Colorado. Her bags were packed, but her mind raced with questions about the challenges ahead. Sitting in her room one afternoon, she stared at a text from Colonel Hales: *"Tough days are coming. But remember why you're there. Keep pushing, even when it feels impossible."* She read it over and over, letting the words anchor her. The drone team had taught her resilience and leadership; now, it was time to prove she could rise to the occasion.

Freddie, meanwhile, was putting the final touches on his flight school applications. Arizona, Texas, South Carolina, and Indianapolis were all in the running, and with each passing day, his dream of becoming a pilot felt more tangible. He thought back to his struggles with calculus and the long hours of tutoring he'd put in. What once felt like a mountain too steep to climb now felt like another step in his journey. "I got this," he told himself, gripping the edge of his desk with steady hands.

Genesis was preparing for a journey unlike any she had taken before. Her mother's recent hire as STEM Analyst at VertiSky brought a renewed sense of stability to their household, a welcome reprieve after months of uncertainty. With that stability came the chance to finally focus on what lay ahead: Tuskegee University. The nine-hour drive to Alabama loomed large, but it wasn't just a trip, it was the start of something monumental.

Over the summer, Genesis had delved into Tuskegee's rich history, learning about famous alumni. Every story she read reinforced her sense of purpose. She wasn't just attending a university, she was stepping into a legacy, ready to leave her own mark.

On their last night together, the trio found themselves flying drones in the Drone Zone, the place where their dreams had first taken flight. The rhythmic hum of the propellers filled the air as drones darted and twirled above them, their LED lights slicing through the early-evening darkness like shooting stars. They raced, looped, and maneuvered through the training course one last time, each of them savoring the moment.

Freddie grinned as he executed a flawless barrel roll. "Still got it," he smirked, eyes locked on his drone's movements.

Miah, never one to back down from a challenge, responded with a perfect zig zag flight. "I don't know, Freddie. I think I just took the lead."

Genesis, ever steady, hovered her drone just above them, casting a soft glow over their faces. "Y'all both know I'm the real MVP," she teased.

They laughed, their banter light, but beneath it lay the unspoken weight of the night.

The realization that this was their final flight together, at least for a while, settled over them like the stillness of the sky.

Freddie leaned against the drone control station, watching as their drones hovered in formation one last time. "Crazy, ain't it? This might be the last time we out here together."

Miah's voice was softer than usual. "Yeah, it's wild. We about to split up, headin' in different directions."

Genesis, ever steady, watched her drone zip through the air, tracing patterns only they could understand. "But distance don't change what we built. What we been through? That stays with us. Always."

They stood there, the weight of the moment heavy but not crushing. Each of them knew this was the end of one chapter and the start of another, but that didn't make the parting any easier.

Miah broke the silence, her voice laced with emotion. "I'm gonna miss y'all so much. It's like… I know we'll keep in touch, but it won't be the same."

Freddie chuckled softly, though his eyes glistened under the drone's blinking lights. "Man, we've been through too much for this to be goodbye. You're my family, no matter where life takes us."

Genesis smiled faintly, her calm confidence shining through. "We said it before, and I'll say it again, we gonna fly. Together. Don't matter how far apart we are."

For a while, they simply stood there, watching their drones dance against the backdrop of the city. The lights seemed to twinkle just for them, a reminder of the endless possibilities that lay ahead.

When it was finally time to leave, they powered down their drones and packed up their gear with a shared resolve, their movements deliberate and steady.

Their paths were taking them in different directions, but they knew their bond was unbreakable. They had built more than a team, they had built a legacy. At U-Street High School, they had shown what could be achieved with grit, heart, and a shared dream. And now, as they prepared to soar into their own futures, they carried that legacy with them, ready to inspire others to rise and reach for the skies.

30

LEVEL UP

Miah's first few weeks at the Air Force Academy were nothing short of brutal. Days started before dawn, filled with grueling drills, relentless physical training, and an unforgiving mental grind that left her questioning everything. The routines were unyielding, the expectations towering. Each stumble, each missed mark, was met with sharp corrections and a reminder of the Academy's high standards. And for the first time in her life, Miah found herself doubting whether she had what it took.

One scorching afternoon, she faced an obstacle course that felt more like a gauntlet. Each hurdle seemed designed to break her, crawling under barbed wire, scaling towering walls, and dragging weighted sleds across uneven ground. Her muscles screamed with every movement, her breath shallow and uneven. Halfway through, she faltered, collapsing onto her knees. For a moment, defeat loomed, whispering that she wasn't strong enough.

But as she sat there, her mind replayed the memories of the national drone competition. She saw Freddie, his steady hands on the controls, determined to lead the team forward despite the odds. She thought of Genesis, her calm voice guiding them through setbacks, always finding a way to keep them on track. She remembered the way they had all rallied when things seemed lost, leaning on each other's strengths to rise above.

If we made it through that, I can make it through this, Miah told herself. With a deep breath, she forced herself back to her feet. The voices of her teammates echoed in her mind, their belief in her driving her forward. Slowly, deliberately, she tackled the rest of the course, her legs burning but her resolve unshaken. When she crossed the finish line, the wave of relief was accompanied by pride. She had pushed herself further than she thought possible.

That night, as she lay on her bunk, exhaustion weighing her down, her phone buzzed with a message from Freddie. He was just starting his flight school journey, and his words struck a chord.

> *"Learnin' to trust myself more every day*
> *Whenever I'm behind the controls, I think*
> *of you and Genesis. You guys believed in me, so*
> *now I believe in me too   ."*

Miah stared at the message, a tired but genuine smile spreading across her face. Across the miles, their bond remained a lifeline. They were all facing their own battles. Freddie in flight school. Genesis carving out her place at Tuskegee. But they were still connected, drawing strength from the lessons they'd learned together.

By the time the final week of training arrived, Miah had transformed. The physical demands no longer felt insurmountable, and her mental resilience had sharpened. She tackled every drill with the same determination she'd found leading her drone team, each obstacle a reminder of how far she'd come. When the day of the final evaluation arrived, she stood at the starting line, nerves buzzing but her focus razor-sharp.

The evaluation pushed her to the edge, every sprint, climb, and crawl felt like it was designed to test her limits. But she didn't falter. She channeled every ounce of strength and grit she had, and when she crossed the final line, the weight of triumph washed over her. She hadn't just survived; she had conquered.

As she stepped off the field, sweaty and exhausted, her heart swelled when she saw her parents waiting for her. Her dad, who had once doubted her dream, now wore an expression of pure pride. Her mom's eyes glistened with tears as she wrapped Miah in a tight hug.

"You did it," her mom whispered, her voice thick with emotion. "You showed everyone what you're made of."

Her dad pulled her into a strong, steady embrace, holding on just a little longer than usual, his silent way of saying how proud he was.

Miah held onto her dad tightly, her voice steady despite the lump in her throat. "I couldn't have done it without y'all, or without Freddie and Genesis. They're with me every step of the way."

As Miah stood there, the sense of accomplishment sank in. She wasn't just stepping into her future; she was soaring toward it, carrying the lessons of her past and the unshakable belief that she could conquer whatever came next.

31

CLEARED FOR TAKEOFF

At flight school in Myrtle Beach, South Carolina, Freddie was living his dream, at least on the surface. Each successful flight felt like a triumph, especially with his favorite instructor, Mr. Jaleel Johnson, often praising his composure under pressure. But one hurdle loomed large, casting a shadow over his progress: the check ride, the ultimate test that would determine whether he was ready to earn his private pilot's license.

This wasn't just another flight. The check ride was the culmination of all his training. Navigation. Emergency procedures. Technical skills. Each performed under the watchful eye of an examiner. Every misstep could mean failure. While his instructors believed in him, Freddie wasn't sure he fully believed in himself.

As the day approached, doubt crept in like an unwelcome passenger. Sleepless nights were filled with mental drills and second-guessing every detail. His conversations with Miah and Genesis had helped in moments of clarity, but the pressure was building.

On the evening of the check ride, Freddie arrived at the hangar early. He ran through the pre-flight inspection with trembling hands, muttering under his breath, "Trust your training. You've got this." The familiar rhythm of the checklist steadied him, but the nerves simmered just below the surface.

His examiner, Mr. Taylor, a seasoned pilot with a no-nonsense demeanor, greeted him with a firm handshake. "Ready to show me what you've got?" he asked, his tone calm but weighty.

Freddie nodded, forcing a small smile. "Yes, sir," he replied, though his heart was pounding in his chest.

The check ride began with the oral exam, a grueling series of questions about weather patterns, airspace regulations, and emergency scenarios. Each question felt like a puzzle Freddie had to solve on the spot. He remembered Genesis' words from weeks earlier when he'd called her in a panic: "You've studied this, Freddie. Trust yourself, you know what to do."

Repeating her words like a mantra, Freddie methodically worked through the questions. When Mr. Taylor finally nodded and said, "Let's see how you fly." Relief washed over him. Brief, but enough to carry him to the next phase.

The cockpit felt like both a haven and a test chamber as Freddie settled in. The familiar hum of the engine grounded him, and he took a deep breath as he guided the plane onto the runway. The takeoff was smooth, and as the plane ascended, the anxiety began to melt away. This was his element.

The first tasks were straightforward, steep turns, stalls, and slow flight. Freddie's movements were precise, his training taking over. Then came the simulated engine failure, the test he'd feared most. The sound of the throttle pulling back filled the cockpit, and for a moment, his heart raced.

"You've got this," he whispered to himself, channeling Genesis' voice.

He followed the emergency checklist step by step, guiding the plane into a safe descent. Mr. Taylor's approving nod bolstered his confidence as they continued.

By the time they reached the final phase, night flying, Freddie felt a steady rhythm in his movements. But when Mr. Taylor requested an emergency approach in the fading light, the tension ratcheted up again. Stay focused, Freddie told himself. The darkness outside was disorienting, but he locked his attention on the instruments, trusting his training.

As the wheels touched the runway with a smooth bump, a flood of relief coursed through him. They taxied back to the hangar, and Freddie waited in silence as Mr. Taylor scribbled notes on his clipboard. The moments stretched on, each second filled with anticipation.

Finally, Mr. Taylor turned to him, his expression breaking into a rare smile. "Congratulations, Freddie," he said, his tone warm. "You're officially a private pilot."

The words hit him like a tidal wave. All the doubts, the sleepless nights, the grueling hours of study, they had led to this moment. Freddie had done it. He was a licensed pilot.

That night, he couldn't wait to share the news. He FaceTimed Miah and Genesis, his grin nearly splitting his face. "Yo! I did it. Ya boy is officially a licensed pilot!"

Miah let out a loud cheer, and Genesis clapped, her face lighting up with pride. "Freddie, that's amazing!" Miah said. "I knew you had it in you."

"Of course he did," Genesis added with a smirk. "But now you owe us a flight someday."

"You already know I got both of you," Freddie replied, laughing.

As he ended the call and looked out at the night sky, Freddie felt something shift inside him. He had taken on his biggest challenge yet and proven to himself that he could rise to any occasion. The journey ahead was still vast, but now he felt truly ready to take it on.

32

EMBRACING LEADERSHIP

At Tuskegee University, Genesis was thriving in ways she never expected. The coursework was demanding, but she welcomed the challenge, knowing each late-night study session, each hour in the flight simulator, and every moment in the cockpit brought her closer to her dream. The campus buzzed with history, its rich legacy weaving through her daily routines. Walking the same paths as aviation pioneers reminded her, she was part of something far bigger than herself, a legacy she was determined to honor.

One afternoon, after a grueling meteorology for aviation class, Genesis made her way toward Moton Field to log her flight hours. The sun cast long shadows across the historic airfield, and as she approached the hangar, Captain Titus Sanders, the director of the aviation science program, caught up with her. His expression was thoughtful, his tone warm.

"Genesis," Captain Sanders began, his voice steady and encouraging, "I've been keeping an eye on your progress, and I'm genuinely impressed. You've got a natural focus and dedication that stand out. With that in mind, I'd like to offer you a new challenge, one that could take you beyond your individual achievements. How would you feel about stepping into a leadership role within our student aviation organization?"

Genesis froze, the words catching her off guard. Leadership? She had always been a diligent student and a steady teammate, but she had never seen herself as someone who led from the front. Her mind flashed back to her days on the drone team, where she had quietly supported Freddie and Miah, content to be the glue holding things together.

"I don't know if I'm the right person for that," she admitted hesitantly, her voice soft. "I've never really thought of myself as a leader."

Captain Sanders offered her a knowing smile. "Leadership doesn't always mean being loud or commanding attention. Sometimes, it's about influence, the quiet kind. I've seen how your peers turn to you for advice, how you handle challenges with composure. That's leadership, Genesis. You've already been doing it; you just haven't claimed it yet."

That evening, Genesis sat in her usual corner of the library, Captain Sanders' words repeating in her mind. The dim light reflected off the stacks of aviation manuals and study guides around her. She stared out the window at the campus lights twinkling against the deepening night, her thoughts drifting back to the moments that shaped her.

She remembered calming Freddie's nerves during drone competitions, offering encouragement to Miah when setbacks threatened to derail them, and guiding younger students who admired her focus and determination. The realization hit her quietly but profoundly, she had been leading all along, just not in the way she had imagined.

The next day, she accepted Captain Sanders' offer, stepping into a new role she was both excited and nervous about. The first few weeks were chaotic as she learned the ropes of organizing meetings, guiding projects, and mentoring her peers.

There were moments of self-doubt, but Genesis leaned into the quiet strength she had built over the years. Her steady, thoughtful approach quickly earned her respect.

One day, as her team worked to finalize a fundraiser for an upcoming aviation project, tensions flared. A disagreement over the budget turned into a heated argument, with voices rising and frustration mounting. Genesis, feeling the weight of her new role, took a deep breath and stepped forward.

"Hey," she said firmly, her voice cutting through the chaos. "Let's take a step back. We're all here because we want this to succeed, right? Then let's focus on finding the best solution, together."

The group fell silent, her words sinking in. Slowly, they began to work through the issue with a renewed sense of collaboration. Watching the project come together, Genesis felt a quiet pride. She wasn't leading by commanding attention; she was leading by listening, guiding, and keeping the team grounded.

That evening, she called her mom, her voice tinged with both pride and disbelief. "Mom, I took on a leadership role today," she said, her words spilling out in a mix of excitement and nerves. "And you know what? It feels... different. Not in a bad way, just not what I thought leadership would be."

Her mother's voice was warm and steady. "Genesis, you've always had that strength in you. It's about time the world saw it too. You're making us all proud."

As she ended the call, Genesis stood for a moment, looking out over the campus bathed in the glow of the setting sun.

Her chest swelled with a sense of purpose. Becoming a pilot was still her dream, but this was about so much more. It was about honoring the legacy of those who came before her and paving the way for those who would come next.

33

THE LEGACY CONTINUES

Back at U-Street High School, the drone club had transformed into a powerhouse. What had once been an overlooked after-school activity with a handful of students had grown into a thriving program, buzzing with energy and packed with eager participants. Freddie, Miah, and Genesis had left more than trophies behind, they had sparked a movement. Their journey inspired not just the school, but the entire community, setting the stage for a new generation of dreamers to rise.

Mr. Barlow stood at the edge of the gym-turned-drone-zone, watching as students moved between stations. The hum of drones filled the air, accompanied by the excited chatter of kids strategizing over their flight paths. The club now boasted sleek new equipment, a cutting-edge flight simulator, and enough funding to participate in regional and national competitions. But what made Mr. Barlow smile most wasn't the high-tech gear, it was the drive he saw in the students. The same spark that had carried Freddie, Miah, and Genesis through their journey was alive in this new wave of pilots.

One afternoon, as a group of new recruits gathered for their first practice, Mr. Barlow spotted a young girl struggling with her controls. Faith, a freshman with sharp eyes and a determined expression, was hunched over her drone's controller. Her brows knit together in frustration as her drone clipped a cone and wobbled to the ground.

"Dang, I'll never get it," she muttered, biting her lip.

Mr. Barlow walked over, crouching beside her. "Hey, Faith," he said softly, "you know, when Freddie first started, his drone crashed almost every session. Genesis? She used to panic during the tight turns. And Miah, well, she nearly walked away after her first drone spiraled into a fence."

Faith glanced up, her frustration giving way to curiosity. "Really? But they're, like, amazing now. They're pilots."

Mr. Barlow nodded, his eyes kind. "They are, but they didn't start that way. They made mistakes, got frustrated, and sometimes wanted to give up. What set them apart was that they kept coming back. Every crash was just another chance to learn."

Faith looked back at her drone. The doubt in her eyes faded, replaced by something steadier. Hope. "Do you think... I could be like them? A pilot?"

Mr. Barlow's voice was firm but gentle. "I don't just think it, I know it. You've already taken the hardest step by showing up and trying. The rest is just practice, perseverance, and believing in yourself. One day, Faith, you'll be the one inspiring others."

As Faith picked up her drone and returned to practice, her movements steadier this time, Mr. Barlow took a moment to soak in the scene around him. The club had come a long way from its humble beginnings, those early days of patchy equipment and small competitions felt like a lifetime ago. Yet, the essence of what made it special remained the same: it was a place where students discovered their potential, supported one another, and dreamed bigger than anyone thought possible.

He could still see traces of Freddie's intense focus, Miah's unyielding determination, and Genesis' calm strength in the students' faces. Their legacy wasn't just etched in trophies or victories; it lived in the spirit of the club itself. Every flight, every challenge, every dream was a continuation of the foundation they had built.

Faith's drone took off again, wobbling slightly before finding its rhythm. It climbed higher this time, steady and determined, cutting through the air with purpose. Mr. Barlow smiled, watching her face light up with pride.

The legacy was alive, thriving, and preparing the next generation of leaders, aviators, and innovators. U-Street's drone club had become more than just a program, it was a symbol of resilience, ambition, and the power of possibility.

EPILOGUE
SOARING TOGETHER

Years later, Freddie, Miah, and Genesis found themselves reunited, this time at an aviation gala in Chicago, held at the breathtaking Willis Tower, 110 stories above the bustling city. The event, hosted by AeroStar Avion Institute, celebrated individuals who championed youth aviation, and the trio stood among the honorees, recognized for their groundbreaking contributions.

Miah had risen to the rank of Lieutenant Colonel, a celebrated Air Force fighter pilot known for flying critical missions and mentoring the next generation of cadets, especially young women breaking barriers in the military. Freddie, now a Captain for a major airline, dedicated himself to mentoring aspiring pilots from communities like the ones he, Miah, and Genesis came from, ensuring that more young people could see a future in the skies. Genesis had emerged as a leader in the aviation industry, founding a nonprofit that provided scholarships and mentorship to future innovators from diverse backgrounds, all while serving as a First Officer at a regional airline.

Standing under the spotlight, the warmth of applause washed over them. Miah felt her heart tighten, her vision blurring as tears threatened to spill. Freddie stood tall, shoulders squared, his jaw clenching as pride and gratitude surged through him. Genesis' eyes shimmered, a tear escaping before she quickly brushed it away, her smile unwavering. The soft murmur of conversations mingled with the faint melody of jazz drifting through the room, wrapping them in an atmosphere of celebration.

The applause swelled, echoing like a heartbeat, as they accepted the prestigious Dr. Tammera L. Holmes Legacy Award, an honor recognizing trailblazers who broke barriers by establishing transformative aviation programs and mentoring talented youth from across the country. A ripple of emotion passed through the group as the weight of their journey settled in, the triumphs, the losses, and the dreams that had carried them here.

Among the audience were aspiring aerospace professionals, young dreamers who mirrored their younger selves, brimming with hope and determination. Miah, Freddie, and Genesis had become the role models they once longed for, living proof that with unwavering determination, resilience, and a shared commitment to uplifting others, no dream was too far out of reach.

Dr. Tammera L. Holmes, founder of AeroStar and affectionately known as the "Aviation Queen," dedicated her life to breaking barriers and creating pathways for countless students to dream bigger, work harder, and achieve greatness in aviation. Through transformative initiatives such as mentorship programs and aviation education starting as young as kindergarten, she directly impacted thousands of young minds, inspiring many to pursue careers once thought out of reach. Her legacy of "Giving Wings to Dreams" not only inspired the trio but also shaped the very foundation of the evening's celebration, serving as a beacon for a future where the skies reflect a rich tapestry of perspectives and hold no limits for those bold enough to dream.

After the ceremony, they slipped away to the observation deck, where the city's lights stretched endlessly below. The wind carried the faint hum of traffic from the streets, and the stars above seemed to wink knowingly, as if acknowledging their journey. The three of them leaned against the railing, the vast cityscape before them, a canvas of possibilities.

Genesis broke the quiet first, a sly grin spreading across her face. "You'll never believe who I ran into last week."

Miah turned to her, intrigued. "Who?" Genesis let the suspense build before finally saying, "Big Rodney." Freddie perked up. "Big Rod? No! What's he up to these days?" Genesis snickered. "He's Director of Aircraft Maintenance for an airline."

Freddie let out a short laugh, shaking his head. "After all the smoke he gave me about aviation and now he's in the industry. That's wild."

Miah arched a brow. "Guess he was paying more attention than we thought."

Genesis nodded. "He told me Mr. B had him fixing all the old drones, and he ended up really liking it. Mr. B saw his potential and helped him enroll in an aviation maintenance program after high school."

"Wow," Miah said, shaking her head. "Mr. B really looked out for all of us."

Freddie smirked. "Yeah, but I still can't believe Big Rod, of all people, is in charge of repairing airplanes now."

Genesis chuckled. "Life's funny like that. He's also helping U-Street start an aviation club with a financial literacy component for students and families, and I'm gonna help."

"Yo, that's a great idea!" Freddie said. "I want in on that."

"Yeah, me too." Miah added.

"I'll let him know," Genesis said casually.

Freddie tilted his head, grinning. "Wait... you two talk pretty often now, huh?"

Genesis smiled. "We've shared a few texts, that's all."

"That's cap!" Freddie said, eyes wide with amusement. "Come on, G, you know that's cap. You like this dude, don't you? Miah, you know about this?"

"Leave me outta this!" Miah threw her hands up.

"Oh, so you knew," Freddie said, pointing at her dramatically.

Genesis rolled her eyes, laughing. "Hey, Fredrick, mind ya business, man!"

The three of them burst out laughing.

Suddenly, a server passed by with a tray of drinks. Freddie waved him down, his grin easy and familiar. "Got any sparkling cider for a few tired dreamers?"

The server chuckled, holding up the tray. "It's all apple cider tonight. Figured it'd keep the celebrations sweet."

"Perfect," Freddie said, grabbing three glasses and handing one each to Miah and Genesis.

He lifted his glass, his voice steady, carrying a quiet pride. "To all the dreams we thought were too big to reach."

Miah raised hers with a knowing grin. "And to proving everyone wrong who ever said we couldn't. Especially Cameron." Her eyes danced with mischief as she rolled them playfully.

Freddie shook his head with a chuckle. "Miah, Cameron's your husband. He's literally in the ballroom right now, sitting at your table."

Miah's laughter spilled out, light and unrestrained, echoing into the night. "And he's still cute."

Genesis' gaze moved to the shimmering stars above. Her voice was soft but carried a quiet strength. "This is for Mr. B," she said. "He always told us that the only limits we have are the ones we set for ourselves. Here's to being his Urban Wings."

They all raised their glasses, the crystal catching the starlight. For a moment, silence settled over them, each heart carrying a piece of Mr. B's wisdom. The glasses clinked, the sound echoing like a shared promise, a vow to keep dreaming, to keep climbing, and to always pave the way for others.

A breeze whispered around them, carrying the city's hum and the echoes of laughter from the gala below. Someone wiped a tear, another nodded in silent agreement. Then, as if on cue, their laughter filled the night, weaving memories of challenges faced, victories earned, and lessons learned. Under the vast sky, they stood together, united by the past, inspired by the future.

Freddie leaned back, his eyes tracing the endless skyline. "We've come a long way, but I think we're just gettin' started."

Miah smirked, nudging him playfully. "Of course we are. The skies are too big to stop now."

Genesis' quiet smile softened as she glanced at her friends. "And we're not just flying for us anymore. We're flying for everyone who comes after."

They stood at the edge of a world they had once only **imagined**, the breeze whispering promises of endless possibilities. The sky stretched before them, painted in hues of gold and amber, a canvas as limitless as their future.

From that first rooftop, where they had longed for a future beyond their reach, to this moment, standing as leaders and as inspirations, their journey had come full circle. Everything they had fought for, every challenge they had overcome, had led to this moment.

Together, they had proven what their mentor had always instilled in them: there were *no limits, just skies.*

Darrell E. Morton Jr. is a multifaceted aviation professional and certified FAA sUAS pilot who serves as a Part 107 Test Prep Instructor drone flight test proctor. With a passion for empowering future innovators, he is on a mission to inspire the next generation of dreamers and doers in drone technology, aviation, aerospace, and the fast-moving world of urban mobility.

A historian of early Black aviation history preceding the Tuskegee Airmen, Darrell is dedicated to preserving and sharing the often-overlooked stories of pioneering aviators. As a Senior Manager at a regional airline, his leadership played a key role in expanding aviation pathway programs for students from communities with limited access to industry opportunities. Notably, he played a key role in helping Tuskegee University relaunch its historic flight training program at Moton Field, home of the legendary Tuskegee Airmen. Because of his outreach and advocacy, two-thirds of the students in the inaugural Aviation Science cohort, launched on January 6, 2025, were directly influenced by his efforts.

A U.S. Army veteran, Darrell holds a Master's degree from Ball State University and a Bachelor's degree from Indiana State University. He brings discipline and focus to every endeavor, whether leading educational initiatives or officiating as a Division I college baseball umpire, demonstrating calm, fairness, and precision in high-pressure environments.

Darrell is also a published author whose U-Street series blends real-life challenges with aspirational narratives. His most recent book, *Urban Wings: No Limits, Just Skies*, continues the legacy of his earlier works: *Report Card Daze*, *Bully on the Bench*, *Freddie at the Plate*, and *Airplane Mode*. Through his writing, Darrell uses storytelling as a powerful vehicle to educate, uplift, and inspire youth to dream beyond the horizon.

Other books by Darrell E. Morton, Jr.
available on

amazon

Get Involved!
Ready to take flight with drones or aviation? Link up with an organization and start your journey.

Youth-Serving Aviation Organizations	
AeroStar Avion Institute	avioninstitute.org
AngelCity Aerospace	angelcityaerospace.org
Alabama Aerospace and Aviation High School	alaahs.org
Archer Youth Programs	archeryouthprograms.org
Aviation USA	aviationusa.net
Aviation Youth Mentoring Program (AYMP)	aymp.world
Buckeye Tigers Aviation Programs	buckeyetigers.com
Fly Compton Aero Club	flycompton.com
Future Aviators Charitable Foundation (FACF)	futureaviatorsfoundation.org
Infinity Aero Club	infinityaeroclub.org
Latino Pilots Association	latinopilot.org
NAYR Foundation	nayrfoundation.org
Operation Aviation Foundation (OAF)	operationaviation.org
Organization of Black Aerospace Professionals (OBAP)	obap.org
RedTail Flight Academy	redtailflightacademy.org
RedTail Scholarship Foundation	rtfa.org
Sisters of the Skies	sistersoftheskies.org
Skyward Youth Aviation	skywardyouth.org
Stand & Serve	standandserve.org
Teens-In-Flight	teensinflight.org

The Omar Brock Foundation, Inc.	thebrockfoundationinc.com
The 99th Squadron	the99th.org
Tuskegee NEXT	tuskegeenext.org
Urban Aviators Society	urbanaviatorssociety.org
Urban Wings and Aerospace Leadership Club	urbanwings.club
Youth Eagles Aviation & Aerospace Education	youtheaglesaviation.org

Youth-Serving Drone Organizations

Black Boys in Tech (BBIT)	blackboysintech.org
Black Girl Drone World	blackgirldroneworld.com
Crew Concept	crewconcept.co
Drone Cadets Foundation	dronecadetsfoundation.org
Drone Force Indiana (Drone Force America)	droneforceindiana.com
Drone Legends	dronelegends.com
Drone Together	dronetogether.com
Droneversity	droneversity.org
Drones 4 Kids	drones4kids.org
Drones In The Classroom	dronesined.com
Girls STEM Institute	girlssteminstitute.org
Global Air Drone Academy	globalairdroneacademy.org
MultiGP STEM Alliance	multigp.com
Rudder and Compass Essentials Inc.	rudderandcompass.org
STEAM Thru Drones	steamthrudrones.com
U.S. Drone Soccer	dronesoccer.us
VertiSky STEM Solutions	govertisky.com

Want to learn more or get connected with one of these organizations? Visit their websites and take the first step toward getting involved today!

Saluting Those in Aviation, Aerospace, and Beyond
In Gratitude to the Dreamers
Who Inspired This Book

Aaliyah Jones, *Albert T. Glenn*, Alicia Garcia, *Alicia Booker*, Alexis Robinson, *Amayah White*, Amber Grigley, *Amy Arnell*, Ana Garcia-Sanchez, *Anisjah Ballard*, Antione M. Sherfield, *Ashley Gomez*, Avery Taylor, *Alvaro Ramirez Davila*, Ayah Muhammad, *Ben Brown*, Bernadette Monk, *Bisher Nimri*, Brenna Daniels, *Brandi Fox*, Brandon Frisso, *Bradley Murphy*, Brenden Fenner, *Brelis Spiller*, Brian Hughes, *Bryan Bedford*, Bryson Beaver, *Brigadier General (Ret.) William L. Sparrow, U.S. Air Force*, Carl Richards, *Carlos Nelson*, Cetrena Simmons, *Chauntal Ledgister*, Chris Barlow, *Christian Copeland*, Christopher "Frozone" Williams, *CJ Charlton*, Chauncey Spencer II, *Cilia Salam*, Colleen Kennedy, *Colonel (Ret.) Al M. Niles Jr., U.S. Army*, Colonel (Ret.) Richard Toliver, U.S. Air Force, *Colonel (Ret.) Roosevelt J. Lewis, U.S. Air Force*, Courtney Kendrick, *Craig Hurd*, Cynthia Park, *Damon Benson*, Darryl Wyrick, *David E. Brown*, David Dorsey, *David Lyles-Holly*, Dean Dube, *Debbie Watson*, Demel Bolden, *Dennis Jarrett*, Derrick Wilkerson, *Devon Watson*, Di Copelin, *DiAndre Harrell*, Douglas Veverka, *Dominique A. Scott*, Dr. Aleesia Johnson, *Dr. Ashley McIntyre, M.D.*, Dr. Charity Garcia, *Dr. Crystal H. Morton*, Dr. Charlotte Morris, *Dr. Farrah Ward*, Dr. Heidi M. Anderson, *Dr. Kuldeep Rawat*, Dr. Kimberly Slater-Wood, *Dr. Larry Nulton*, Dr. Larry Young, *Dr. La'Quata Sumter*, Dr. Lynda Brown-Wright, *Dr. M. Javed Khan*, Dr. Mark Brown, *Dr. Patrcia Payne*, Dr. Ric Fowler, *Dr. Robyn Murphy*, Dr. Rolundus Rice, *Dr. Ruth Woods*, Dr. S. Keith Hargrove, *Dr. Tammera L. Holmes*, Dr. Terrance Fountain, *Dr. Theodore W. Johnson*, Dr. Vann R. Newkirk, *Ebony Searcy*, Ella Puran, *Emily Munoz*, Eric Goshay, *Eric Hendricks*, Eric Rosa, *Eric Whisler*, Eric Vetro, *Erwin Salazar*, Ethan Fehl, *Faith White*, Fatima Johnson, *Flack Maguire*, Frank "Chris" Lee, *Gary Naylor*, Gentry Hudson, *Genesis Santana*, Glenn Ponas, *Gordon Fykes*, Grace Cantwell, *Israel Reid*, Ivan Blount, *Jailah Long*, Jaleel Johnson, *Jalen Goshay*, James Hashley, *James Tigner*, Ja'Rell Smith, *Jason O. Harris*, Jaxon Trenum, *Jay Shah*, Jeermal Sylvester, *Jeremy James*, Jermaine Morris, *Jerome Lawrence*, Jibri Taylor, *Jim Bogaard*, John Lucas, *John Murray*, Jon Harmon, *Jordan Monk*, Josh Chapman, *Josh Reed*, Jose Ramirez, *Joseph Fleagle*, Joy Murff, *Karent Alejandro*, Karl Minter, *Katherine Caberrra*, Kelly Rynearson, *Ken Elkin*,

Ken Garrett, *Khalid Elhag*, Kimberly Murray, *Krista Saint Dic*, Kushal Patel, *LaQuinta Bester*, La Tonya Stocks, *Leon E. Haynes*, Layla Brown, *Lena Arnold*, Leon Stinson, *Leul Cosentino*, Lisa Quinn, *Lieutenant Colonel (Ret.) Michael Hales, U.S. Army*, Lieutenant Colonel Kenyatta "Deacon" Ruffin, U.S. Air Force, *Lori Lillard*, Lucas Dominy, *Lucille Plummer*, Maenecia Lewis Cole, *Madeline Starr*, Maida Thompson, *Malachi Wattley*, Major (Ret.) Allen Williams, U.S. Air Force, *Markus Jantzon*, Matt Koscal, *Matthew Klein*, Matthew Medley, *Maya Yarbrough*, Mayer Deonarine, *Mayor Tony Haywood City of Tuskegee Alabama*, Michael Johnson, *Mia Hutcherson*, Miah "MJ" Shelby, *Mica Clark*, Miranda Haywood, *Mitchell Carr*, Monica Newman McCluney, *Morgan Rucker*, Myron Braden, *Natalie Mazza Engledow*, Nia Allen, *Nia Spiller*, Nick Williams, *Nicki Robinson*, Nicole Ogbonna, *Nirav Shah*, Noel Ricketts, *Melissa Borom*, Oretes Gooden, *Owen Clencey*, Paula Henrique, *Paul Griffin*, Peyton Alexander, *Phillip Franklin*, Rafael Ramos, *Ramone Crowe*, Ramone D. Hemphill, *Raysean McKoy Marin*, Representative Earl Harris Jr., Indiana, *Resheeda Gates*, Richard "Chubb Rock" Simpson, *Ricardo Foster*, Richard Riley, *Robert Kluck*, Robert Lowe, *Rodriguez F Broadnax*, Ron Thompson, *Ronicsa "Ronni" Chambers*, Ronnel Norman, *Ruben Morris*, Ryan Goertzen, *Ryan Lynch*, Samantha T. Mitchell, *Sandra Patino*, Sarah Defendis, *Sarah Ervin*, Secretary of State Diego Morales of Indiana, *Senator Katie Britt Alabama*, Seneca Garrett, *Shavana Jones*, Shirley Friar, *Simone Williams*, Spencer Edwards, *Stephan Morton*, Stephen Barlow, *Steven Miller*, Susan Kessler, *Sydney Hardeman*, Talmage Turner, *Ta'Lar Cooley*, Tanya Forrest, *Theresa Lester*, Theresa Tardy, *Thonnia Lee*, Thomas Brown, *Tim Simpson*, Timothy O. Johnson, *Timothy Barnett*, Titus Sanders, *Tony Reid*, Tom Merriman, *Tracy Atobatele*, Tracy Gilbert, *Vincent J. McCaskill*, Warren York III, *Xavier Cox*, Xavier Samuels, *Xyrous Cooper*, YaShima Buck, *Yvonne Leggon*, Carlston Elliot, *Crystal M. James*, Neela Sneed, *and the Willa Brown family!*

Schools and Organizations I've Had the Honor of Sharing Aviation & Drone Insights With

ALABAMA

- Alabama Aerospace & Aviation High School – Bessemer
- Tuskegee Airmen National Historic Site – Moton Field
- Tuskegee University Aviation
- Southern Museum of Flight – Birmingham
- Booker T. Washington High School – Tuskegee

CALIFORNIA

- Handle It Helping Hands, Inc. – Fresno
- La Jolla Country Day School – La Jolla
- Quantum UAV Drone Academy – Victorville
- San Bernardino County Superintendent of Schools

DELAWARE

- Delaware State University Aviation – Dover

FLORIDA

- Central Florida Aerospace Academy – Lakeland
- Florida Memorial University Aviation – Miami

GEORGIA

- Hapeville Charter Career Academy High School – Atlanta

ILLINOIS

- Air Force Academy High School – Chicago
- Route History Museum – Springfield

INDIANA

- Boys & Girls Clubs of Indianapolis
- The Children's Museum of Indianapolis
- Frederick Douglass Community Center – Indianapolis
- Indianapolis Public Schools
- Indiana State University – Terre Haute
- Irvington Preparatory Academy – Indianapolis
- Jeffersonville High School – Jeffersonville
- Judah Ministries Inc. – Indianapolis
- KIPP Legacy Academy High School – Indianapolis
- Lawrence Township Schools – Indianapolis
- MLK Center – Indianapolis
- Mount Vernon Community Schools
- The Path School – Indianapolis
- Pike Township Schools – Indianapolis
- Providence Cristo Rey – Indianapolis
- Purdue Polytechnic High Schools (The Lab) – Indianapolis
- Richmond High School – Richmond
- Riverside High School – Indianapolis
- TeenWorks – Indianapolis
- Terre Haute Regional Airport
- Warren Township Schools – Indianapolis
- Vigo County Schools – Terre Haute
- Zionsville Community Schools

KENTUCKY

- Atherton High School – Louisville
- Frederick Douglass High School – Lexington
- Jefferson County Public Schools – Louisville
- Jefferson Community and Technical College
- The Academy @ Shawnee – Louisville

LOUISIANA

- Helix Aviation Academy – Baton Rouge

MARYLAND

- University of Maryland Eastern Shore Aviation – Princess Anne

MISSISSIPPI

- Aberdeen High School – Aberdeen
- Columbus High School – Columbus

NORTH CAROLINA

- Craven County Schools – New Bern
- Elizabeth City State University Aviation

OHIO

- Central State University – Wilberforce
- Cleveland Metropolitan School District
- Columbus City Schools – Columbus
- Dayton Public Schools – Dayton
- Wilberforce University – Wilberforce
- Withrow High School – Cincinnati

PENNSYLVANIA

- Aerium – Johnstown
- Hosanna House – Wilkinsburg
- String Theory Schools – Philadelphia
- The School District of Philadelphia

SOUTH CAROLINA

- Richland County Schools – Columbia
- Williamsburg County Schools – Kingstree

TENNESSEE

- Memphis East T-STEM Academy
- Memphis Shelby County Schools

TEXAS

- Dallas Independent School District
  - Cedar Crest Elementary School
  - John Lewis Social Justice Academy at Oliver Wendell Holmes
  - Thomas Jefferson High
- Everman Independent School District - Everman
- Houston Independent School District
- Region 10 Education Service Center - Richardson
- Texas Southern University Aviation - Houston

VIRGINIA

- Hampton University Aviation - Hampton
- Thomas C. Boushall Middle School - Richmond

WASHINGTON

- Grand Coulee Dam School District - Coulee Dam

WEST VIRGINIA

- Barnes Learning Center - Fairmont

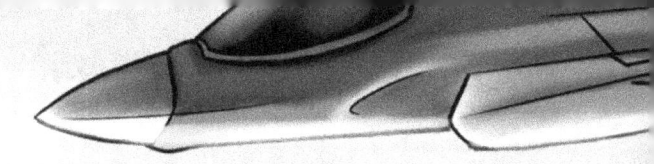

"Inspiring 500,000 young people across the globe to pursue careers in the drone, aviation, aerospace, and urban mobility industries."

-DMJ

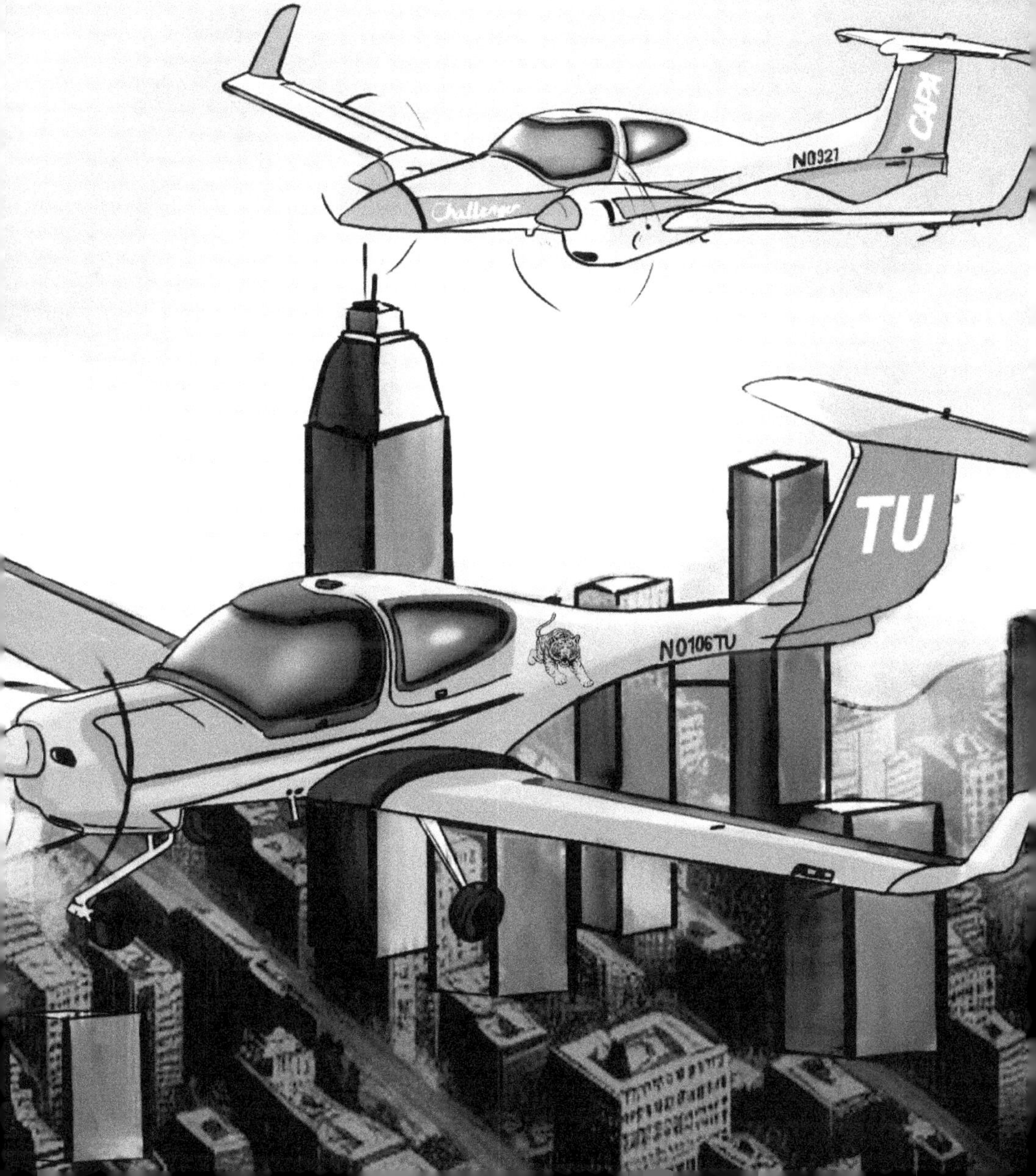